"A choice to deceive her mother leads to devastating consequences for Cleo as her life spirals out of control. Honest and direct, Melody Carlson infuses her words with insight and sensitivity and creates a challenging story that will have teens contemplating the crushing impact of keeping a deadly secret. *Shattered* is a powerful tale of tragedy, grief, and guilt as a young woman journeys through unimaginable pain in search of forgiveness and healing. Highly recommended."

—REL MOLLET, book reviewer, Relz Reviewz,
www.relzreviewz.blogspot.com

"*Shattered* is a powerful story that will bring you to tears. Melody captures the emotions of a girl ridden by guilt and grief after one poor decision. You'll find a message of hope and redemption that's riveting and life-changing."

—SUSAN CHOY, The Reading Mom, Five Star Reviewed Books
and MORE

"*Shattered* is an unflinching, realistic portrayal of grief, hope, and healing. A must-read for teens"

—KATHLEEN FULLER, author of *A Summer Secret*,
*A Hand to Hold*, and *The Secrets Beneath*

# SHATTERED

## A Daughter's Regret

Melody Carlson

Discipleship Inside Out™

**NAVPRESS**

Discipleship Inside Out™

NavPress is the publishing ministry of The Navigators, an international Christian organization and leader in personal spiritual development. NavPress is committed to helping people grow spiritually and enjoy lives of meaning and hope through personal and group resources that are biblically rooted, culturally relevant, and highly practical.

**For a free catalog go to www.NavPress.com**
**or call 1.800.366.7788 in the United States or 1.800.839.4769 in Canada.**

© 2011 by Melody Carlson

ISBN-13: 978-1-60006-949-9

Cover design by Faceout Studio, Charles Brock
Cover image by iStockphoto.com

Published in association with the literary agency of Sara A. Fortenberry.

Some of the anecdotal illustrations in this book are true to life and are included with the permission of the persons involved. All other illustrations are composites of real situations, and any resemblance to people living or dead is coincidental.

Library of Congress Cataloging-in-Publication Data

Carlson, Melody.
  Shattered : a daughter's regret / Melody Carlson.
      p. cm. -- (Secrets ; 2)
  Summary: Seventeen-year-old Cleo, feeling guilty that her choices played a role in her mother's murder, seeks refuge in prescription medication until her Aunt Kellie helps her to tell the truth and find some perspective.
  ISBN 978-1-60006-949-9
  [1. Death--Fiction. 2. Guilt--Fiction. 3. Drug abuse--Fiction. 4. Grief--Fiction. 5. Aunts--Fiction. 6. Christian life--Fiction.] I. Title.
  PZ7.C216637Sim 2011
  [Fic]--dc22
                                    2010037811

Printed in the United States of America

1 2 3 4 5 6 7 8 / 15 14 13 12 11

*Helicopter Mom* is a phrase that must've been coined to describe my mom. I am convinced of this. Oh, she would never admit to hovering or overprotecting or smother-mothering me to the point of near asphyxiation. If anyone suggested such a thing, her response would be to flash an effervescent yet innocent smile and say, "It's simply because I love Cleo so much, and I only get one chance to be a good mom." And thanks to Mom's sunny disposition and sweet spirit, most would excuse her bad behavior.

Even I used to excuse her. Like the time she was the only parent to show up at the middle school assembly where ex-cons were talking to students about "stranger danger." I was a little red-faced then, but I knew she meant well. And after she heard their sincere presentation and was assured that they weren't actually using the assembly as an opportunity to pick out their next young victims — namely, me — she went home and made brownies. I forgave her then . . . and many times afterward.

But the older I got, the less tolerant I grew. And now, as a healthy, normal seventeen-year-old girl who wants some independence, here is what I know for sure: If I look over my shoulder, my mom will most likely be there. Lurking somewhere on the sidelines or in the shadows, she will be watching (aka spying) to ensure that "nothing goes wrong in my life."

It's not exactly that she doesn't trust me. It's just that she's certain without her constant attention, supervision, intervention, and assistance, my life will be completely derailed by some invisible force intent on destroying me.

"What about prayer and trusting God?" I've challenged her from time to time. My mom's a churchgoing Christian who firmly believes her Bible, and I'm always hoping the faith track might gain me some ground.

"I *do* pray and trust God," she's told me. "But I can't expect him to do everything, Cleo. God gave me the important job of being *your mother*, and that means I look out for your best interests." And so it goes.

But on a Friday morning in mid-April, I am ready to draw a line in the sand with my mom. After all, I'm nearly eighteen, I'm a senior, and next year I will be going away to college. So I inform her that my best friend, Lola, and I plan to attend a concert this evening.

"What kind of concert?" she asks with a look of alarm.

"A *Christian* concert." I hope the emphasis on *Christian* will reassure her.

"Oh . . ." She nods like she's processing this. "So is it at church then?"

"No . . . it's at the Coliseum."

Her brown eyes get bigger. *"In the city?"*

"Yes, Mom, as far as I know, the Coliseum is still in the city."

"How are you getting there?" Her brow creases.

"I hoped maybe you'd let me drive Dad's car."

She laughs like this is really funny. "Oh, Cleo, you've got to be kidding."

"I'm totally serious."

"You honestly think I'd let you drive Dad's car, or any car for that matter, *into the city at night*?"

With clenched teeth, I shove my notebook into my bag. I was determined not to lose my temper when I brought up the concert. I wanted to show Mom just how mature I am, how I can be trusted to do something like this. But the truth is, I want to scream right now.

"I suppose I could go with you to the concert," she says in a sweet tone, like this generous offer is going to make my day.

"Right, Mom." I scowl at her. "Seriously, you need to get a life."

"Well, excuse me for trying to help you. I just thought that—"

"I wanted to do this with Lola. She thought she could drive, but her mom needs the car and—"

"Now there is a blessing in disguise! Young girls should not be driving into the city at night. And like I said, I'm perfectly happy to accompany you—"

"This was going to be a special thing for Lola and me," I say firmly. "Lola won the tickets on the radio, and it seemed like a God-thing—"

"Are you saying God wants you and Lola to drive into the city at night, all by yourselves?" She looks at me like I'm still seven, like she's imagining a little girl behind the wheel of a car, driving off to what will be certain death.

"I'm not a child, Mom."

"Yes . . . I know, Cleo. But you're not an experienced driver, either."

"I'm a good driver!"

"Maybe so, but you've never driven in the city, dear."

"And whose fault is that?"

She shrugs. "Look, sweetie, I said I would go with you. Isn't that good enough? And if it makes you feel better, I don't even have to sit with you girls."

"We don't need a chaperone, Mom." Still standing, I pick up a glass of already poured orange juice. "But if you want to drop us off and pick us up, maybe that would be okay."

"Fine." She nods in a way that convinces me she still plans on actually attending the concert with us. "So the concert's Saturday night, right?"

"No, Mom." I take several gulps of juice, then reach for a piece of raisin-bread toast. As usual, despite that Dad's on a business trip and it's just Mom and me, she's made enough breakfast to feed a family of six. "I told you the concert's *tonight*. Lola just won the tickets yesterday and — "

"Is that all you're eating?"

Ignoring this, I point at today's date on the calendar on the fridge. "And you know as well as I do that it's your friend's bachelorette party tonight."

Mom frowns. "I thought you might want to come with me."

"I don't even know her."

"But she'd love to meet you, Cleo."

I roll my eyes. "Yeah right, Mom. I'm sure on the eve of her wedding, she is dying to meet your teenage daughter."

"But she was one of my best friends in college."

"Which is exactly why you don't want to miss her party and why you should let me use Dad's car. In fact, if you're that worried about me driving in the city, maybe Lola could drive."

Mom's look is all the answer I need. No way is she going to let Lola drive Dad's beamer into the city.

I take a bite of toast, then nod to the clock. "I gotta go, Mom."

"Take this too." Before I can leave, she grabs a carton of yogurt from the fridge and pushes it at me.

"No, I'm fine with juice and toast."

"Oh, Cleo." She frowns, as if I might expire from hunger before lunch.

"Later, Mom." I hook the strap of my bag over one shoulder, blow her a kiss, and zip out the door.

Feeling slightly defeated, I hurry toward Lola's house. I hadn't expected Mom to roll over on this, but I had hoped for some sort of compromise. Maybe after school I can talk her into dropping us off before the party and picking us up afterward. I'll play the sympathy card, reminding her that this is the last night for me to be with my best friend.

As I get closer to Lola's house, just six houses down from mine, I feel excruciatingly sad. I can't believe this is Lola's last day at school. We've been best friends since eighth grade, and in less than three months we would've been graduating together. But Lola's world got turned upside down last summer when her parents divorced. And then Lola's mom, Vera, lost her job shortly before Christmas. She got herself a headhunter and was finally offered a position in San Diego a few weeks ago — and they are moving tomorrow.

Now I realize Vera desperately needs this job, but I still don't get why she wouldn't let Lola stay behind and live with me until graduation. Well, aside from the fact that Lola helps to babysit her twin brothers after school, which in my opinion is totally unfair. In fact, I was so upset when Vera put her foot down, saying there was no way Lola would get to stay with me, that I told her so.

"I don't understand how you can be so selfish," I told Vera after she'd shot down my idea.

Okay, I wasn't exactly being respectful, but I was too exasperated to care. Plus, Vera is the kind of person who speaks her mind and usually encourages others to do so too. And I was fed up. I'd witnessed Vera taking unfair advantage of Lola for years. Like when the twins were born seven years ago, Lola automatically turned into a live-in nanny. And after Lola's dad left, things only got worse.

"That's just because you're an only child," Vera told me after I'd calmed down from having a small hissy fit. "And because you're spoiled."

"I am not spoiled."

She just laughed at me. "Your mother does everything for you, Cleo. I'll bet she even makes your bed."

"She does not!" Okay, the truth is she does sometimes, but I was not going to let that cat out of the bag.

"And she chauffeurs you to ballet like you're a prima donna. And she probably still cuts the crusts off your bread —"

"You're nuts!"

She sighed. "I know you love Lola and you want her to be a spoiled prima donna just like you, but that's just not going to happen."

I tried other tactics, but Vera was not backing down. And then I realized Lola seemed to be resigned to her fate . . . or else she was actually looking forward to relocating to San Diego. Come to think of it, it doesn't sound half bad, considering our so-called spring weather has been nothing but gray clouds and rain. Not that I'm admitting this.

Now Lola opens her front door. "Hey, there you are."

"What a mess." I stare at the stacks of boxes and piles of junk and what looks like total chaos behind her.

"The moving van is supposed to be here any minute." She

jingles her keys. "I have to get the car out of the driveway."

"Ready when you are."

"And we don't want to be late."

"That shouldn't matter to you since it's your last day anyway," I say glumly, following her out to the Subaru wagon.

Vera has been letting Lola use her car to drive us to school. That might seem generous at first glance, but it's only to ensure that Lola gets home in time to watch the twins after school. Why Vera can't watch her own kids is a mystery. But Lola is too nice to complain. Oh, that's right; she's not spoiled . . . like me.

"This is so sad." Lola starts the car. "The only thing that'll get me through this day is the concert tonight." She turns and grins. "This is going to be an awesome night, Cleo!"

I don't have the heart to admit that my mom is balking at letting me use Dad's car. Yesterday I assured Lola I could pull this off. But after this morning's conversation, I'm not so sure.

"You still want to go, don't you?" she asks after I don't respond.

"Of course."

"And your mom's letting you use the car?"

I take in a deep breath. "Well . . . we're still discussing it."

"Oh . . ." Her smile fades.

"You know how she is," I say lightly. "She's all freaked about me driving in the city at night."

"Right . . ."

"But I plan to work on her more after school."

"Uh-huh."

"If all else fails, I'm going to guilt her into it," I say with more confidence than I feel.

"That should totally work." Lola's tone is sarcastic now. She knows my mom too well to believe me.

"Somehow we're going to that concert."

"I offered to drop Mom and the boys off at their gig tonight, but she said no way was she going to be stuck at a kiddie birthday party at Fun Town until the concert ends." She sighs. "I kinda see her point."

"Yeah, that does seem a little torturous."

"And if they don't get to go, the boys will throw a fit. And really, it's only fair since this is their last night with their friends, too."

"I'll just have to get my mom to drop us off and pick us up," I tell her.

"She won't mind?"

"I don't think so. Like I said, if necessary, I'll guilt her into it."

"Don't make her feel too bad," Lola says. "I mean, it's not like we *have* to go. We can always just hang at home for our last night. If I hadn't won those tickets, we wouldn't be doing much anyway."

I turn and study my friend. How is it that she's both nice *and* pretty? I can't even imagine how much I'm going to miss this girl! And no way am I going to be the reason her last night here is a washout.

Somehow I have to make my mom understand how important tonight is because more than ever I am determined — *Lola and I are going to that concert!*

ola and I have never been part of the "it" clique, as they like to call themselves. Our rationalization is that we wouldn't want to be as shallow and selfish and mean as those girls anyway. Mostly we keep to ourselves. But we do have a small circle of acquaintances—a combination of some youth group kids, a girl who takes ballet with me, a few "academics," and a couple of Lola's jazz band friends. We're not exactly geeks, but I'm sure the "it" clique likes to think we are. It probably makes them feel more important about themselves. Like they need that.

But one cool thing about our group of friends is they all seem to love Lola nearly as much as I do. And realizing that she won't be around much longer, they're all surprisingly sweet today. At lunchtime we all make a big deal about saying good-bye to her. And Leo Simmons, who I'm sure has been crushing on her for years, buys everyone ice cream in Lola's honor. I think she is touched.

"This was a great day," she tells me as she drives us home.

"Great and getting greater." I smile.

"Maybe for you, Cleo. I have to go home and help Mom clean up our house. That should be fun."

"Do you want help?" I offer halfheartedly.

"No, that's okay."

"Yeah, I should probably focus my energy on my mom."

"Do you really think she'll agree to drive us?"

"I'm 99 percent sure." That's an exaggeration, but I'm trying to think positively.

"Cool." Lola is all smiles as she stops in front of my house. "I can't wait."

"I'll call you later." I reach for my bag. "That way we can coordinate what we're wearing to the concert. And maybe you can spend the night at my house, too."

"Sounds good. Especially considering we were going to sleep on the floor tonight anyway."

So I wave and get out of the car. I'm sure I can convince Mom to taxi us tonight. I will begin with sweet talk, and if that doesn't work, I'll move into guilting mode.

"Hi, Mom," I say cheerfully as I come into the kitchen. "Did you have a good day?"

She looks up from where she's writing something in a card. "I did. And how about you?"

"It was kind of rough seeing Lola's last day at school." Then I tell her about how we had an impromptu party for her at lunch.

"That must've been nice." She slips the card into the envelope.

"But Lola's still feeling pretty bummed. It's so hard for her to leave all her friends and everything . . . so close to graduation."

My mom nods with a sympathetic expression. "It's too bad for Lola. But I know Vera feels fortunate to have gotten such a great job. She was telling me a little about it today. It sounds like a wonderful opportunity for her."

"Anyway, I told Lola that you could probably drop us off at the concert tonight and pick us—"

"Why did you tell her that?" Mom's brow creases.

"Because we talked about it this morning, *remember*?"

"You mentioned it, Cleo, but I never agreed to anything."

"But you could drop us off before you go to your party. You could just go into the city and—"

"Except that Trina's bachelorette party is in Riverside."

"Couldn't you drive us to the city and then go to Riverside?" I plead.

Her mouth twists to one side in a way that makes me brace myself. This is her *sarcastic* expression. Like she's about to say something in jest. "Well, let's see, Cleo. It's almost an hour to get into the city, longer during rush hour." She holds up one finger. "And it's an hour to get back here." She holds up two fingers. "Then it's another hour to get to Riverside and an hour to get back." She now has four fingers up. "And then it's another hour to get back into the city again." She looks at her five splayed fingers and just shakes her head. "Five hours so far. What do *you* think?"

"I think you should let me drive Dad's car."

"You know that's not going to happen."

"But I'm almost eighteen." I'm trying to keep my voice even. "You have to let me grow up sometime."

She smiles a bit smugly. "Yes, dear. And that's exactly why I'm saying no to driving your dad's car into the city tonight. Because I want you to grow up and live to a nice ripe old age." She picks up the newspaper and holds it up, as if it holds some mysterious kind of explanation.

But I don't even look at the paper. Instead I stare at her. "Mom, you *have* to let us do this. It's Lola's last night, and she won the tickets, and it's a Christian concert. Honestly, what could possibly go wrong?"

She shakes the newspaper, pointing to a headline. "Look at this, Cleo. There was a shooting on Wednesday night. Right down there near the Coliseum, and a young man died and—"

"There will always be something," I say a bit too loudly. "There will be car wrecks and epidemics and murders and all sorts of horrible things happening all over the planet, Mom. But that does not mean they'll happen to me. Don't you get that? Someday you will have to let me go!"

"I know . . ." She nods sadly. "But I do not have to let you go into the city tonight."

*"Mom!"*

"I'm sorry, Cleo, but everything in me says this is a bad idea."

"You think anything I want to do without you by my side is a bad idea. Seriously, do you plan to go to college with me next fall? Will you be my roommate? Will you walk me to classes? Hold my hand? Wipe my nose?"

She actually looks as if she's considering this.

"You have got to get a life, Mom. Seriously, this is sick and getting sicker."

"I know I'm a little overprotective, but—"

"A *little*? Try *suffocatingly*."

"Oh, Cleo, you're just upset because you're not getting your way."

"It's Lola's last night here." I try to soften my tone. "It's just that I wanted it to be special for her. I want her to have some happy memories."

"Then make a different kind of memory. Make it special for her right here," she suggests. "Isn't it your friendship that matters most of all? Why not invite Lola here for the night? You girls can have the run of the house, and you can order pizza and watch movies and pig out and crank up the music as loud as you like. Now, really, wouldn't that be fun?"

"It might be fun if we were thirteen years old," I snap at her. "But Lola is eighteen, Mom. I'll be eighteen in June. Why can't we do something more age appropriate for a change?"

"It's just not a good night for this, Cleo. Trina's party has been planned for months. Dad's out of town. Vera has her plans. Besides that, she told me they're leaving at sunup tomorrow. I'm sure she'd prefer that Lola isn't out late anyway."

"Vera doesn't care how late Lola stays out," I say with too much anger. "Unlike *some* totally paranoid mothers, Vera trusts Lola. And she doesn't treat Lola like an infant."

Mom presses her lips together, and I can tell she's mentally counting to ten. But I just stand there with my hands on my hips, glaring at her. I'm so mad that my fingernails dig into my palms. Why does she have to be like this?

"I suppose I could cancel on Trina's party," she says sadly. "That way I could take you girls to the concert."

Suddenly I'm wondering who is guilting who now? "No way. I won't let you do that, Mom. Then you'll blame me for missing out on the one thing you've been looking forward to for ages."

She holds up her hands. "Then what do you expect me to do?"

"I don't know." I turn away from her, ready to throw something or just scream. Juvenile? Yes. But isn't that how she's treating me?

"I wish you could see that it's for the best, Cleo. It's really not safe for two young girls to drive into the city, park down by the Coliseum, and walk in the dark. If you were older, you'd understand."

"I understand that my mother is a total freak. A controlling, fearful, obsessive freak who is always expecting disaster to strike."

She blinks. "I'm sorry you feel that way."

"And I'm sorry you're my mom," I snap back. "I wish I was an orphan!" I complete my juvenile act by stomping off to my room and slamming the door so hard the wall shakes. I pace back and forth in my room now, feeling like a caged tiger, ready to claw and bite and tear into any unsuspecting thing that dares to open that door. Fortunately, my mother doesn't make any attempts.

After a while, I quit pacing and just sit on my bed. What is wrong with that woman? Okay, I am fully aware that my mother grew up in a very dysfunctional home. A crummy little house in a run-down neighborhood with too many kids and not enough supervision. Her parents were both flaming alcoholics. Her dad barely held a job. And her mother walked out on her husband and five children when my mom was only twelve. As the oldest daughter, my mom had to play "mommy," trying to hold the family together, but it was a thankless and impossible task. It was a rough way to grow up, and I do feel for her. But that was then; this is now.

It doesn't take a shrink to figure out that my mom has over-compensated for her sad upbringing by creating what she considers a perfectly safe haven here in our home. After putting herself through school and working in real estate for years, she married my dad in her midthirties. She waited until she was nearly forty to have children, and then she had only one—me. Driven to "do this right," she gave up her career to stay home and play mommy. She made it her full-time job to take care of me.

So really, I'm not stupid. I know exactly why she is the way she is, and most of the time I try to be tolerant. But for some reason — maybe it's losing Lola — I'm completely out of patience today. I'm fed up. I feel the walls closing in on me, like I can't breathe, like something's got to bend before it breaks into a million little pieces.

I need to take my life into my own hands. Seriously, it's about time!

So with a fresh rush of independence flowing through my veins, I go online and check out other options for getting into the city tonight. I quickly discover I'm too young to rent a car and a taxi is too expensive. But then I remember there's a bus stop a couple of blocks away, and upon closer investigation, I discover this very bus line connects to the metro that, as fate would have it, has a stop *right in front of the Coliseum*. How safe is that?

Now I'm tempted to go present this new liberating information to my mom, except I *know* my mother. She would see danger around the corner. She would throw a complete fit if she thought her child was going to use *public transportation*. Good grief, the woman freaks out when I use a public restroom. And to ride the metro (with all those thugs and drug pushers) into the city in the dark of night — well, I might as well pick up a gun and play Russian roulette! So I decide to take a different route with her. I don't want to lie, but it will be a sort of "don't ask, don't tell" policy. I won't give her a chance to ask and I won't tell.

I return to the kitchen, but she's not there. I look around the house and finally find her in her bedroom, getting dressed for tonight's big bash. She looks surprised to see me. I'm sure she thought I'd pout for much longer than an hour.

"I'm going to Lola's," I say in a defeated sort of way. "She said they can use some help cleaning up the house."

Mom gives me a forced-looking smile. "Oh, that's nice of you, Cleo. I wish I could help too, but I'll need to head out of here by five in order to make it on time."

"Yes, it's nice that *someone* gets to do what she wants tonight."

"Oh, Cleo." She shakes her head at my snarky tone as she takes a black-and-white striped dress from the closet. She's had that dress for years, probably since the previous century. She holds it up in front of the mirror, studying her image with an unhappy expression.

I'm tempted to tell her to choose something else, but why bother? If she wants her friends to tell her the eighties are calling and have decided they want their dress back, what's it to me?

"Have fun," I say in a flat way that suggests I won't be.

"Are you going to invite Lola to spend the night tonight?" she asks hopefully. "Order pizza? Watch movies?"

I shrug. "Maybe . . ."

"I'm sorry about the concert, Cleo, really I am."

"Yeah, I know," I say glumly. I figure the less I say, the less I will have to lie.

"And I'll fix you girls breakfast in the morning. In fact, why don't you tell Vera to bring the boys over tomorrow? I'll make everyone pancakes and bacon and eggs. Tell Vera I'll have it going really early so they can be on the road before dawn."

"Okay." I'm still keeping up the sad act.

"Oh, Cleo," she says with a frown. "Maybe I should just forget Trina's party and go to the concert with you girls."

"No, Mom." I shake my head. "Go to your party."

"But it's Lola's last night and your last year of high school." She reaches for her cell phone. "And it would be fun to go to a concert."

"No, you need to go to your party."

"But, Cleo —"

"Seriously, Mom." I give her an exasperated look. "Get a life!"

She blinks. "Fine. I'll go to the party."

"Fine," I snap at her, turning away.

As I'm heading down the hall, she calls out that she loves me. Naturally I pretend not to hear. And instead of answering, I just hurry out the front door and away from my house. Maybe by tomorrow, after she finds out it's possible to safely go into the city and return in one piece — and after she gets over being furious with me for doing so — maybe then we can smooth this thing over between us.

In the meantime, I just don't feel like being around her. And really, I wish she would get her own life — and quit trying to run mine.

I've never been much good at housekeeping, but I try to make myself useful at Lola's, which is something of a joke. And it's not long before Lola asks me to take the twins to the neighborhood park.

"We'll need to be ready to leave for the concert before six," I tell her.

"But the concert doesn't start until seven thirty."

"I know, but we need to leave my house *before* six."

She gives me a curious look, but I'm already herding the boys out the door. "We'll be back here by five thirty sharp," I tell her. "Then we'll go to my house to get ready. *Okay?*"

She nods. "Okay."

"Race you guys to the park." I take off running with the twins at my heels. To my surprise, either Jamie and Eddie have gotten faster or I've gotten slower, and they easily beat me. Thanks to some of their friends who are already there and kicking a soccer ball around, all I'm required to do is supervise and cheer.

While I'm standing there, I go over tonight's scheme, trying to decide whether or not it will really work. And suddenly I get what I think is a brilliant idea . . . or a really dumb one.

Sometimes the line between smart and stupid is very narrow.

But before I can question myself, I call my mom's number. Because it's a bit past five, I'm pretty sure that (1) she'll be on her way to Trina's party and (2) she will not answer her phone because she's extremely diligent about never using her phone while driving. To my relief, I go straight to her voice mail. Taking in a fast steadying breath, I begin. "Hey, Mom, we had a slight change in plans. Lola is so sad about moving and leaving her childhood home that we decided to spend her last night at her house—kind of campy, but it'll be fun."

Then as I close my phone, I crystallize the final part of the plan. When we get home from the concert, I'll tell Mom we changed our minds and decided to spend half the night at Lola's and half at mine. For some reason I think this might work, keeping my mom from ever knowing we went to the concert. Or maybe I'll just confess and hope that Mom won't flip out with Lola around.

At five fifteen, I yell to the boys that it's time to go. Naturally they don't want to leave the fun, but when I remind them of the birthday party they're going to tonight, they're suddenly racing me back to their house.

Soon Lola and I are leaving her strangely empty house, but before we go, Vera asks where Lola's sleeping tonight. "After the concert will you stay here or at Cleo's?"

"I'll let you know," Lola says.

Suddenly, I feel uneasy. What if my lies catch up with me? I'd hate for Lola's last night here to be spoiled by my mom throwing a fit. But Lola is eager to spend the night in a real bed, so I agree. Then as we're walking to my house, she asks me if we're taking my dad's beamer.

"I wish." I explain my alternative plan of using public

"Did you already put your phone on silent mode?" Lola asks me as she's turning hers off.

"Good idea." I reach into my bag only to discover my phone's battery is dead. I can't believe I forgot to charge it this afternoon, especially considering how we're out traveling around and about the city tonight. But at least Lola's phone works. Still, I can only imagine what my mom would say if she knew. And, of course, this just makes me start thinking about my mom again.

I try to focus on the music, to enjoy the concert, but this evening seems to be contaminated by a nagging feeling of guilt. As hard as I try to push it away, it's like an obnoxious little dog that keeps nipping at my heels. And it doesn't help when the lyrics we're rocking out to involve concepts like truth and integrity. Still, this night is about Lola. I'm doing the best I can to make it special for her. And by tomorrow it'll all be just a memory—a really fun memory.

As we listen to a song about forgiveness, I decide I will absolutely confess what I did to Mom . . . eventually. After I've given her enough time to get over being angry, she'll *have* to forgive me. So really, it's not such a big deal. I just hope (and pray) we have no problems getting home tonight.

As the concert's winding down, I glance at my watch to see it's well past ten o'clock. Commuting home on the metro and transit bus at this late hour might be different than traveling in the daylight.

But as we exit the Coliseum, I keep my concerns buried deep inside me. No way do I want Lola to know I feel worried. I don't want anything to spoil this evening for her. We get on the metro, and it's obvious that the commuters at this time of night are a bit different from the ones we saw earlier.

The woman opposite us looks tired or perhaps even sick.

She's clutching a raggedy purse and a plastic bag with her eyes downward. Or maybe she's asleep. A couple of guys in the back of the car look a little scary. In fact, I'm sure my mom would assume they were "druggies," as she sometimes calls them. An older guy near us definitely has a dark look about him, like he's angry at the world. Still, I could be all wrong. These people might just be down and out and Jesus still loves them.

"Should we talk in French again?" Lola whispers to me in a way that suggests she might be a bit nervous, too.

I consider this but then question the idea of appearing to be tourists with this kind of crowd — what if they perceive foreigners as an easy target? "Maybe not." I sit straighter. Then I attempt to make small talk with her, hoping to distract us and pass the time.

Finally it's our stop, which looks relatively tame in the middle of our sleepy town, except Main Street is dark and pretty much deserted since it's past eleven now.

"The bus still runs, doesn't it?" Lola asks with wide eyes.

We check the schedule and discover that it does run, but only until midnight. "I'm glad we got here when we did," I tell her.

She nods. "It'd be a long walk home."

Soon we're on the bus, along with a couple of questionable-looking people. But I remind myself not to be judgmental. Just because someone looks like a thug doesn't necessarily mean he is a thug. I realize how influential my mom's overly cautious attitudes have been on me. And I hope that I can overcome some of my unreasonable fears before I go to school next fall. Parents really should be more careful about the paranoia and phobias they pass on to their kids.

It's nearly midnight by the time we make it back into our neighborhood. Although I'm relieved to be back, I feel exhausted from the long evening, which seems ironic since it was supposed to be fun. Although in some ways it was pretty cool . . . it had its moments. And I think Lola had a great time.

But, for me, tonight was like a tainted layer cake. First was a layer of guilt from knowing I've disobeyed my mom, the next layer was stress (worrying that something could go wrong on our way to or from the concert), and the final layer was the anxiety of how my mom will react when she eventually finds out. Although I don't plan to confess for a day or two. Unless she somehow found out already. It's possible that the icing on this spoiled cake will be when we walk in the door and my mom makes a huge scene and ruins the whole evening for Lola.

In fact, I'm tempted to suggest that Lola spend the night at her house after all, except her stuff is already in my house. Plus she doesn't even have a bed to sleep in, and I have a perfectly good spare trundle bed in my room. So, bracing myself, I unlock the front door and tiptoe inside.

"Maybe my mom's already gone to bed," I whisper to Lola.

She nods like this makes sense, and I'm thinking there is no way my mother would be sleeping if she knew where I was tonight, so perhaps it's a very good sign that she's oblivious. Some of the lights are on, and there's a small hot-pink gift bag on the breakfast bar, which must be from the bachelorette party, so I know Mom's home.

Putting my forefinger over my lips, I tell Lola to keep quiet on her way to my room. "I'll get us something to snack on."

Before long we're safely tucked away in my bedroom with root beer and tortilla chips and Mom's homemade salsa, and I'm feeling relatively relieved—like we're *home safe!* I'm so happy I'm almost giddy, and it turns out that neither of us feels very sleepy.

"I'm going to set my phone to wake me up at five thirty," Lola tells me.

I groan. "That early?"

"Yeah, Mom wants to hit the road before six." She sighs. "I can't believe this is our last night, Cleo."

"I wish your mom would let you stay here."

"You'll come visit me in San Diego after graduation, won't you?"

I nod eagerly. "Yeah, if I can talk Mom into it."

We talk awhile longer, then decide to watch one of our favorite movies, which I pop into the DVD player. But it's not long before I can hear Lola making sleeping noises and I feel like I'm nodding off too. I turn off the TV and am about to say my usual bedtime prayer, mostly telling God what I'm thankful for and the usual stuff, but I realize it would be wrong to thank God for letting me slip beneath my mom's radar tonight. So I don't pray at all. I promise myself to make up for it tomorrow.

It seems like I'm barely asleep when Lola taps my shoulder. "I gotta go," she whispers.

I blink into the gray dawn light. "What time is it?"

"Almost six."

I sit up in bed and we hug each other, and I can tell Lola's crying and I feel like crying too except I'm barely awake. "Have a good trip, Lola."

"I'll call you later today," she promises. "Or when we get there. But that won't be until late tonight."

I hug her tightly. "I'll miss you!"

"Me too." And then she wipes her nose and tiptoes out of my room.

It always takes me a while to wake up, and by the time I'm finally fully awake, I wish I'd walked Lola outside, stood on the curb, and waved good-bye. But when I hurry out to do this, I'm too late. Their car is gone . . . their house looks abandoned and empty. They are gone.

Now I cry. I stand there staring at the house, feeling like I've just lost my best friend. Then I realize it's true; I sort of did just lose my best friend. Maybe not permanently. But it still hurts.

I return to my house, tiptoeing back into my bedroom. I close the door and climb into my bed, which is still warm, and decide to sleep in as long as possible. I know part of my rationale is that I am postponing the inevitable — confessing to my mom that Lola and I snuck off to the concert last night. Or maybe I'm hoping my procrastination will somehow soften the blow.

Still, I remind myself as I'm drifting off, *Mom has to forgive me.*

## CHAPTER 4

I'm shocked at how late I am able to sleep in. It's 11:40 by the time I finally crawl out of bed, which is a personal record for me. But I can't believe Mom hasn't been in here to wake me up yet. That's so not like her. Or maybe she thinks I'm still at Lola's, though that makes no sense. Whatever the case, I'm beyond ready to get up. However, I'm not sure I'm ready to face the music quite yet. Although it might be best just to get this thing over with—the sooner the better.

I wander out of my room, thinking I'll just spill the beans and get it out in the open. I'll contritely confess my transgression and beg her to forgive me. I'll even offer to do some household chores as punishment. And I won't protest if she grounds me. It's not like there'll be much to do with Lola gone anyway.

But Mom doesn't seem to be around. The house looks exactly like it did last night. It also seems strangely quiet. I go into the kitchen and am surprised to see that Mom hasn't made coffee yet. And the hot-pink bag is still sitting on the breakfast bar, just like it was yesterday. I peek inside to see chocolates and some other goodies, and I'm sure it's a party favor from last night.

I look for Mom in the laundry room, the family room, the

backyard; I even go down to the basement. This is a space my mom renovated for me when I was in grade school, complete with a hardwood floor she installed herself, a wall of mirrors, and a ballet barre. I'm expected to spend an hour practicing on weekdays, which I skipped yesterday, but I can make up for it this weekend. Maybe I'll put in three hours today as a form of penance. Of course, Mom isn't down here. I don't know why I thought she would be. I turn off the lights, promising myself to return after I eat some breakfast.

But as I go up the stairs, I get a bad feeling in the pit of my stomach — like something is wrong. Is Mom okay? What if she's sick in bed? Perhaps she even cried out for my help, but I was sleeping so soundly I didn't hear her. I'm sure there was drinking at Trina's party, but my mom is a teetotaler, a social drinker who sips ginger ale in a wine glass in a pretense of imbibing. So it's not like she'd be suffering a hangover the way Lola's mom sometimes does. Still, Mom could've eaten a bad piece of fish or caught a flu bug or perhaps she tripped and sprained something.

I tiptoe down the hall to the master bedroom and tap on the door. When no one answers, I feel seriously concerned. "Mom?" I crack open the door. Her bed is neatly made and nothing looks amiss. I figure she simply got up early and made her bed, perhaps even made coffee, then cleaned everything up and went out somewhere. I should've thought to check the garage for her car.

Trina's wedding isn't until tonight, but maybe she had to run out and get something for the wedding. Maybe new shoes. My mom could use a new pair of shoes. Only I wish she would've asked me to go with her. She's a little fashion challenged sometimes, and I like helping her out.

Before I leave her room, I check the master bath where, as

usual, everything is in place. I just shake my head at the perfection here. This is a skill I have so not mastered. Finally I go peek in the garage to discover her car is gone. She's obviously out doing something. Although it's weird she didn't even leave a note. She is a stickler for notes. But maybe this is a step toward independence — for both of us. As I return to the kitchen and pour myself a bowl of Cheerios, I remember how I told her yesterday to get a life. Maybe she's just trying to teach me a lesson.

Then as I'm finishing my cereal, I remember something Mom said yesterday. She wanted to fix a big breakfast for Lola's family this morning. And it's not like her to forget something like that. Why didn't she at least come into my room to wake me up? Or even if she thought I was spending the night at Lola's, she surely would've called to see if we were coming over for breakfast. Wouldn't she at least call my cell phone?

Naturally that reminds me of my dead phone battery. So I head back to my room to recharge it and have barely plugged it into the outlet when the doorbell rings. For some reason, which makes no sense, I'm thinking that must be Mom — like maybe she forgot her key, which is ridiculous since my mom never forgets anything. Except that it seems she forgot her promise to fix us all breakfast this morning. So who knows?

But when I open the door wide, instead of my mom I see two uniformed policemen. State policemen. I just stare at them. What are they doing here? Do they think I called 911? Or did I do something wrong? Well, besides lying to my mom about last night's concert, which I'm sure isn't considered breaking the law or a punishable crime.

"Is this the home of Karen Neilson?" the taller policeman says in a serious tone.

I nod. There's a strange uneasiness in the pit of my stomach.

"Are you a relative of Karen Neilson?"

"She's my — my mom," I stammer. "Is something wrong?"

"Is your father at home?"

"No. He's away on — on a business trip." I look from one solemn face to the other as they introduce themselves in a way that suggests I should pay attention, but their names go right over my head.

"What's going on? *Where's my mom?* Is she okay? Was there a car accident?" My heart is pounding so hard that I can feel it thumping in my ears. I know something isn't right. *"Where is she?"*

"May we come inside?"

I step back now, moving away from the front door, and somehow I lead the two policemen into the living room. But my legs feel shaky, and when one of them eases me down to the couch, I don't resist. "What's wrong?" I ask in a voice that sounds small and weak. "Where's my mom?"

"There's no easy way to say this," the shorter man tells me. "Your mother has been the victim of a murder and — "

"The victim?" I interrupt him. "What do you mean? Is she in the hospital?"

He shakes his head. "No, she didn't survive the — "

*"What are you saying?"* I stand. "What do you *mean?"*

The tall cop helps me to sit down again, and then they take turns telling me about how my mother was in the wrong place at the wrong time, how there have been "a string of drug-related crimes . . . a series of senseless murders in this particular neighborhood . . . carjacking, theft . . ." But their words are disjointed, floating over me — all I can think is that *this is a big mistake.*

"*Who* did you say was murdered? Are you sure it's *my* mother? I really don't think it could be my mother. I mean, my mother is a very careful person. She would never go anywhere dangerous. And besides she came home last night and——"

"Is your mother here?" the short policeman asks.

"Well, I can't find her," I admit with a shaking voice. "But I know she was here. She must've left on an errand this morning. So I'm sure you've got it all wrong."

"This is the right address, the right name on her ID," the short guy explains. "We found it in her purse."

"Her purse?" I swallow hard, looking from one man to the other. "You have my mom's purse?"

The tall officer gets up. He takes out his phone and heads back toward the door. Maybe he's going to check his facts better. Perhaps he's really got some other woman's purse. And really, policemen shouldn't go around upsetting people with false information like this.

"Because I know my mom," I say urgently. "She is the last person in the world who could be in the wrong place at the wrong time. She is a very cautious woman. You have it all wrong. You've made a mistake." I stand now, like I want to see these guys out the door. Let them go to someone else's house and tell someone else her mother has been murdered, because I know it couldn't happen to my mom.

The short policeman looks slightly bewildered. "I know this is hard to hear, Miss Neilson. But I assure you that——"

"How do you know what you're talking about? You don't even know my mom. This has to be a mistake. Maybe someone stole my mom's purse and her ID, and she's——"

"The victim matched the ID. Of course, we'll need a positive identification from a friend or family member. When will your father be home?"

"My dad! I need to call him right now. He'll make you understand this is a mistake." I hurry to the phone, dialing his cell phone number with trembling hands. Feeling shaken and slightly numb, I wait to hear his voice.

*"Dad!"* I cry shrilly into the phone.

"Cleo? What's wrong?"

"You have to talk to these men — "

*"What men?* What are you talking about?"

"These *policemen,* Dad. They're in our house and — "

"Why are they in our house? *What is going on?* Where's your mom, Cleo? What's — ?"

"That's just it — they're saying — they're saying — " And I break into sobs. "They're saying it's *Mom* and that — that she's been *murdered*!"

*"What?* What are you talking about? *What is — ?"*

"I — I don't know, Daddy. I — I think they — they got it wrong. It must be wrong . . ." I fall apart now, sobbing so hard I can't speak. The short policeman takes the phone from me, and I collapse onto the couch mumbling, "You got it wrong . . . It's wrong . . . all wrong . . . I know you're wrong." But even as I repeat these words over and over, as if saying them makes it so, I have this horrible, ugly, unbearable feeling deep inside that what they are saying is really true.

*My mother is dead.*

As a woman named Marsha talks to me, I feel like I'm not really here. I'm sitting on the couch in my living room, but it's like I'm not. She's been talking to me about grief, but I feel like she's speaking to someone else.

"Do you have a relative or friend?" she asks with a worried brow.

"Huh?" I stare blankly at her. Is her hair real? Is it as stiff as it looks . . . a bad case of helmet hair . . . a strange shade of blonde . . . kind of greenish yellow . . . or maybe it's just me.

"A grandparent? Or an aunt? A neighbor?"

"Why . . . ?" I squint at the sunshine coming through the blinds. Mom usually tips them up by this time of the day. She worries that the direct light will bleach the dark green couch.

"Someone you can stay with," Marsha explains. "A friend perhaps?"

"My best friend moved away today," I say in a flat voice that doesn't even sound like me. "And now they tell me my mom is dead." I begin to cry again. My head hurts from so much crying, my throat feels raw and sore, and my eyes burn. I want to sleep for a long time . . . and wake up from this nightmare later.

"Officer Lake told me your father should be home sometime

before midnight. Do you think you'll be okay until then?"

I just look at her. Doesn't she get it? I will never be okay again . . . *ever*.

"Or I can arrange for someone to come over and stay with you until then. We have volunteers who are happy to step in and help."

I turn away from this woman with weird hair. I want her to leave. I don't want her strangers coming into my house.

"I know this is very hard for you, Cleo. And I really don't want to leave you alone like this. Are you sure you don't want to come to the —"

"I don't want to *go* anywhere," I say for what feels like the tenth time. "I want to stay here. And I'm not a child. I do not need a babysitter."

"No, I'm sure you don't. But you are very upset. And it's understandable. I really hate to leave you alone like this."

"Please, go." I try to force some life back into my voice. "Really, I will be okay. I just need to deal with this in my own way. *Please*."

"Well . . ." She stands and shakes her head. "You do have my card. I hope you will call me if you need anything. If not today, perhaps tomorrow or next week."

"Yes." I stand too. "I'll do that."

She looks at me as if she knows I'm lying. But then she picks up her purse or briefcase or whatever it is and leaves. And now I am alone. Really alone.

She's barely driven away when the phone rings again. It's been ringing like this about every five minutes. And instead of picking it up, I just let it go to the answering machine. This time it's Dad's golfing friend.

"Hugh, this is Glen. I just heard something terrible on the

news. Was it really true? Is that Karen Neilson your wife? I sure hope not. But call me, man, tell me what's up. And remember I'm here for you, buddy."

I turn the volume way down on the answering machine, then head for my room, which still looks trashed from last night — dried-up salsa, tortilla crumbs on the rug, soda cans, unmade beds. But I turn off the light, close the drapes, step over the trundle, climb into bed, pull up the covers, and take in a jagged breath. My head is still throbbing, pulsating behind my eyes, ringing in my ears. I close my eyes and begin counting backward from a thousand.

When I wake up, it's to the sound of my cell phone ringing, and for a moment I forget . . . and then I imagine I've been having a bad dream. But then I answer my phone, and I can hear it in my dad's voice. This is real.

"Are you okay?" he asks with so much concern that I know I'm going to start crying again.

"I . . . I don't know."

"I'm in shock too, Cleo. But I'm about to board the plane. I just wanted you to know."

"Yeah . . ."

"I have a connection in Chicago with a three-hour layover. I'll get it changed if I can. Otherwise it'll be after eleven by the time I get to the airport. And I'll just get a taxi to bring me home."

"I could pick you up."

"No, I don't want you driving into the city at that hour. Not after what . . . well, you know."

"Yeah. Okay."

"I wish I was there for you, Cleo. I just can't believe this . . . It feels like a nightmare."

"I know. I keep wishing I'd wake up."

"I love you, honey."

"I love you too, Daddy."

"Hang in there."

"You — you too." My voice cracks.

"I'm coming home."

"I know." Then we both say I love you again and hang up. I've never been really close to my dad. I know he loves me — and I love him — but he's always traveled so much with his work, and Mom was always the one there for me. I sit on the edge of my bed, staring at my phone and trying to make sense of this madness, lining up the facts as if they are numbers. Numbers that should all add up.

My mother is dead.

She was murdered by strangulation.

Her body was spotted early this morning by a jogger who immediately called 911.

Several hours later, detectives found her purse, minus credit cards and cash, in the bushes nearby.

Her car, now reported stolen, is still missing.

Estimated time of death is between ten and midnight last night.

But it's the location of this incident that made me so sick to my stomach that I vomited several times already.

My mother's body was discovered in Riverside Park, a strip of greenway that borders the river running through the city, *right next to the Coliseum.*

It doesn't take a genius to guess what my mother was doing there last night. Still I need to know. I push the key to access my voice mail; afraid to breathe, I listen to the female electronic voice telling me, *"You have four new messages —"* Before she can finish her sentence, I push the key to listen to my messages. The first one is recorded at 7:49 p.m. Friday. It's from my mom, but I clench my teeth as I hear her speaking—she sounds very upset.

"*Cleo!*" Mom's voice is tight but controlled. "*I just spoke to Vera and she informed me that you and Lola have gone to the concert! She thought you took Dad's car, which you know you were forbidden to do. I'm leaving Trina's party right this minute. I am getting into my car and going home. If you get this message, I expect you to do the same.*"

The next message is also from my mother, about an hour later, but she's still agitated. "*Cleo, while I am slightly relieved to see that you did* not *take your father's car, I am extremely concerned as to where you and Lola are right now. Vera maintains that you are at the concert, and her guess is that you took the metro to get there. I cannot even imagine you would do something so foolish, but she seems quite sure of it. So I am going to drive to the city and go directly to the Coliseum. It's not quite nine yet, so I expect to get there before ten. I will call you as soon as I arrive so we can plan to meet and I can drive you girls home. I am so disappointed in you, Cleo. I cannot believe you did something so thoughtless. And I can't believe you did it behind my back.* Call me!*"

The third message is from my mother too. "*I'm at the Coliseum. It's 9:53. It doesn't look as if the concert has let out yet. So I will drive around the neighborhood a few times until it gets out. Then I'll see if I can spot you. But please call me as soon as you get this. I want you to call me!*"

I brace myself for the fourth message, but to my surprise it's from Lola. "*Hey, Cleo. We're just stopping for lunch now. Mom's been letting me drive. Last night was so cool. And, oh yeah, Mom says your mom called her a couple of times last night and that she sounded a little worried, but I reminded her that your mom worries about pretty much everything."* Lola laughs. *"Anyway, I miss you already. And I'll try to call you next time we stop, since Mom refuses to let me talk and drive at the same time — even if we're on the most boring straight stretch and there's not a car in sight. Later!"*

And that's it. *"You have no more new messages,"* the electronic voice informs me. I just hold the phone in my hand, staring at it like it's a living thing, like it has the secrets of life inside it. Then I consider replaying my mom's messages again, just so I can attempt to fully wrap my head around exactly what happened last night. But I cannot bear to hear her voice again. Not like that. So frustrated, angry, hurt . . . and disappointed. I don't want to hear the desperate tone of her voice as she begs me to call her back. Besides, I'm pretty sure I know what happened last night . . . and why.

I know who's to blame for my mother's death.

Suddenly I feel like I'm going to vomit again, except nothing's left in my stomach. Even so, I dash for the bathroom and, clinging to the toilet seat, dry heave until it feels like my internal organs are about to come out — and maybe I wish they would. Then finally I collapse, exhausted, on the hard tile floor, curl up into a ball, and just cry.

I wish I were dead.

## CHAPTER 6

Since I can remember, I have always been afraid of the dark. It's not something I'm particularly proud of or something I openly admit to. Lola always had her suspicions, and my dad sort of knows, but my mom was the only one who ever really seemed to understand. Without saying much or making a big deal, she always made sure there were night-lights throughout the house. If a bulb burned out, she would quickly replace it.

But as evening comes tonight, I go around and turn off every single night-light — the one in my bedroom, my bathroom, the hallway, the kitchen, the laundry room. I turn them all off. And then I turn off all the other lights in the house too, until the whole place is pretty much black. Black like I feel inside.

I slowly pick my way through the house now. Finding my way into the living room, I go over to where the streetlight seeps through the cracks in the blinds on the front window, but I close the blinds tight, blocking even that bit of light out. And then I just sit there on the couch . . . in darkness, in the silence. And before long I discover that my fear of the dark is gone. Completely gone.

But instead of feeling relieved, I am disappointed. Almost as if I've been cheated, like one more piece of my life has been stolen from me. Or maybe it's simply been replaced. Because instead of fear, the only thing I feel now is a deep, dark, heavy sense of sadness. It presses down on me like a boulder crushing the life and breath right out of me. I don't know how I can survive this much pain.

Every once in a while I am jolted by the jangling sound of the phone, but I still have the volume on the answering machine turned down so I can't hear any of the messages being left. And anyway, it's like they're all the same, expressing shock and regret over and over like my parents have dozens of close friends and relatives when I know for certain they have few. But it's like everyone is suddenly my mom's very best friend.

Neighbors and people from our church have brought over food. Like they think I can eat. I just nod and take the dishes, listen to them expressing sympathy, and then without asking them into the house, I close the door, take the food into the kitchen, and shove it into the refrigerator. I wouldn't bother to do that except my dad might be able to eat when he comes home.

I'm fairly certain I'll never be hungry again.

I feel dead inside. Dead and hopeless. I wish I could pray. I know I *should* pray. But it's like I don't know how to do that anymore. Like the very act of speaking to a God who could allow something like this to happen is impossible, unfathomable, ridiculous. What would I even say? Would I shake my fist and accuse him of sleeping on the job? Or would I tell him I'm sorry, confessing that my lies cost my mother her life? Would I beg God to take it all back? To turn back the clock and bring my mother back to life? Would I bargain with God? Offer to do what, give what? Even if I could think of something worthwhile, what good would it do? God won't reverse time.

I jump when the doorbell rings. Leaping to my feet and crashing into the heavy oak coffee table, I knock off a bowl of silk flowers and fall onto my knees. I have no idea who is at the door, but for the second time today I get the idea that it could be my mom out there.

I suddenly think that all the events of the day could be just a big mistake, a misunderstanding, or even a hallucination on my part. I feel sure that my mom has come home and she can't find her key, and she'll be standing out there with a sweet but sheepish smile. I flick on a light, rush to the door, and, without even checking to see who it is, fling open the door, fully expecting to see my mother. Ready to hug her, welcome her home, and confess to last night's indiscretion and beg her forgiveness. Instead it's my mom's "slightly functional" sister, Kellie. Clutching her purse in one hand and a hankie in the other. And her eyes are puffy and red.

"*Oh, Cleo!* I heard the news a few hours ago. I tried to call your house several times. And then I decided just to drive over. It's so upsetting!" She grabs me in a bear hug, holding me so tightly I am nearly smothered by her bulky form and overpowering perfume.

After I manage to extract myself from her embrace, I reluctantly let her into the house, which is still mostly dark. Not wanting to explain why the lights are all off, I go around and flip them on, and she follows me, talking the whole time about how awful it is, how unbelievable, until we're both standing in the kitchen.

"I just don't understand it," she says sadly. "Of all people . . . that something like this could happen to my dear sister. Really, she was one of the sweetest people on the earth. *Why Karen?*"

I just shrug. For lack of anything else to do, I fill a glass with water and take a sip. It's lukewarm and tastes metallic, but I don't really care. I slowly sip, focusing on this water as if it's the only thing in the world.

"How are you doing?" She comes closer to me, peering into my eyes as if she expects to spy an answer inside my head.

Again I shrug. "It's been pretty hard." My voice is hoarse and doesn't even sound like me.

"Oh, you poor, poor thing." She comes in for another hug, but I move away, putting the island between us.

"Dad's on a trip," I say stiffly. I glance at the clock and am surprised to see it's almost nine. "He should be home in a few hours."

"Well, I came over here to take care of you," she announces like she thinks I'm five years old and she's Mary Poppins. "I just know that's what Karen would want."

I really want to protest this plan, to tell her I don't need anyone to take care of me, but I simply don't have the energy. So once again I shrug. Then I tell her I'm very tired and want to go to bed.

"Did you eat dinner? I could fix you —"

"Neighbors brought food." I nod to the fridge. "It's all in there. Help yourself."

"Oh . . ."

I turn away and, without even saying good night, go directly to my room and close the door. It's not that I don't like Aunt Kellie. It's just that I don't want her here. With my clothes still on, I climb into bed and slowly count backward from ten thousand.

When I wake, it's dark and silent and I'm not even sure what woke me. But I am wide awake. I look at my digital clock: 2:47.

But I know I can't go back to sleep. So I get out of bed and, tripping over the trundle that is still out, catch my balance on my dresser, then step on a tortilla chip, feeling it crush beneath my bare foot. I can feel all those little pieces being ground into the carpet. Kind of like my life.

I tiptoe out into the hallway and, seeing that the light is on in the kitchen, wonder if someone is still up. Maybe my dad. But when I reach the kitchen, no one is there. Suddenly my stomach clenches. What if something happened to him? What if his plane crashed? Or what if he got mugged on his way out of the airport?

I tiptoe back down the hallway, down to the master bedroom, and silently crack open the door and peer into the darkness. I can't see a thing, but I do hear him snoring. I can't believe what a relief it is to hear that sound. I close the door and go back out into the living room, where I sit on the couch and just stare blankly at the floor.

I realize that until this, I've had a relatively easy life. Nothing really bad has ever happened to me before. Oh, I thought it was hard when I broke my arm the summer I was eleven. It was torture not being able to go swimming, and it seemed to take forever before my cast came off, but eventually that summer came to an end. I was able to return to ballet lessons . . . and life went on.

But this is different. I can't imagine there will ever be a conclusion to this excruciating pain. There is no light at the end of this black tunnel. And I truly don't even care whether or not my life goes on. I simply don't have the energy for it.

I try to remember the things I used to feel passionate about, wondering if anything will ever be worth caring about again. Ballet used to be so important to me. And I had been over the moon about dancing the lead role in June's ballet recital. But now I know I can't do it . . . don't want to do it . . . don't care.

And I used to care about school, making good grades, going to college next year. Now it's unimaginable. Even Daniel Crane, the nicest guy and my major crush who doesn't seem to know I exist, seems uninteresting to me now. Boring even.

I begin to walk through the silent house, absently wandering from room to room, feeling like a stranger in my own home. Or maybe I'm having an out-of-body experience, like I'm not really here at all.

Is this how it feels to be dead? Maybe I really am dead. Maybe I've got this all wrong. Maybe it was me who was murdered last night. After all, I was in the wrong place at the wrong time. Surely it was me who was killed. Not my mom. She would never make a mistake like that.

Yes, I decide, I'm the one who is dead. And now, because I'm not welcome in heaven, I am a ghost destined to walk and haunt this house forever. Yes, it all makes sense.

## CHAPTER 7

"But I really think Karen would want us all to go to church today." Aunt Kellie says this for what seems the umpteenth time. I'm not sure if she thinks we're deaf or just dumb. But I'm pretty sure we've already made ourselves clear on the subject.

"Then *you* go to church." Dad refills his coffee mug. "Because I am not going to church today, and as far as I'm concerned, that's the last I want to hear of it."

"Sorry," I say quietly to her. "I just don't feel like going either."

Aunt Kellie sighs loudly. "Okay, if you're both sure . . ."

Dad turns to me. "I hope I'm not influencing you the wrong way, Cleo. I know your mother probably *would* want you to go to church."

"I think she'd understand given the circumstances."

He nods sadly. "Yeah . . ."

The lump is back in my throat again. Seeing my dad standing there in his bare feet and faded plaid bathrobe, unshaven, dark shadows beneath his eyes, gray messy hair with an ever-widening bald spot . . . well, he just looks so lost and gloomy. And I don't think he's any more pleased than I am that Aunt

Kellie seems determined to park herself in our midst.

She fixed breakfast this morning, but Dad and I both barely touched it. And as she went on and on about what a saint her sister was—and we did not argue—I could tell it was only making Dad feel worse.

As far as I know, my parents never had a romantic fairy tale kind of marriage, but they did like and respect each other. My dad has always traveled a lot for his work, and my mom always tried to make his times at home as easy and comfortable as possible. She'd fix his favorite foods, pick up after him, and when it was time to leave again, she would pack his suitcase with freshly laundered and neatly pressed clothes. She even ironed his boxers.

In fact, Lola was always telling me just how easy my dad had it. Quite a contrast from her mother, where all work was supposed to be shared fifty-fifty, although Vera always complained it was not balanced.

"Your mom totally spoils both of you," Lola would often tell me. I know she was partly jealous and partly amused. But it was true. My mom did spoil us. She cooked, cleaned, did laundry, shopped for groceries, and baked cookies, along with a million other little unseen things I'm afraid both Dad and I never appreciated enough.

"I've got some things I need to attend to today." Dad clears his throat in a way that tells me these are not pleasant things. I suspect he is going to speak to the police, perhaps identify the body, or maybe make funeral arrangements. I do not know and I do not want to know. "Will you be okay while I'm gone?" he directs to me.

I just shrug. "I don't see why not."

He nods as he dumps the contents of his mug into the sink.

The black coffee leaves a dark streak on the white porcelain, which he doesn't even rinse off. Mom wouldn't like that. But she wouldn't say a word either. She would simply scrub it clean and white just as soon as Dad was out of the kitchen.

"Did you check the messages on the answering machine?" I ask him. "There were a lot of calls yesterday. I turned the volume off because I got so sick of hearing them."

"People mean well," he says in a flat tone.

"I guess."

"And I wrote down a couple of messages from this morning," Aunt Kellie informs him. "They're by the phone." She points to me. "One call was for you, a girl named Lola. She said she'd called your cell phone, but you didn't answer. So I explained about your mother."

*"You told Lola?"*

Aunt Kellie blinks at me. "Was there a reason not to tell her?"

"No," I snap at her. "Except that Lola is my best friend and if anyone was going to tell her about this, it should've been me."

"Then maybe you better call her. She sounded pretty upset when I told her . . ."

But I am already on my way to my room. Grabbing my cell phone, I see that Lola has called me several times. I hit speed dial, and she answers on the first ring.

"Cleo!" she cries. "What happened? Is it true what your aunt said?"

"It's true," I say quietly.

*"Oh, Cleo!"* And now Lola is crying, which makes me start crying. And for several minutes we both just sob on the phone.

"I wish I was there with you now," she says in a broken voice. "I told Mom that I wanted to get on a plane and fly right back there, but she won't let me. She says we can't afford it."

"That's okay. There's really nothing you could do around here anyway."

"I could hug you," she says in a slightly hurt tone. "And I could be there for you . . . and listen."

"Yeah . . . I know."

"How did it happen, Cleo? Was it like your aunt said? Was she really *murdered*?"

"Yeah. It happened on Friday night. The night you spent here."

"Wow, and we never even knew about it."

"They didn't discover her—her body until Saturday morning."

"Did her death have anything to do with the bachelorette party?"

"No, it happened after the party. Mom was in her car. The police think it was a carjacker."

"Oh, that's so horrible. Unbelievable. I'm so sorry, Cleo. Is there anything I can do? I mean, besides pray for you. I've been doing that all morning."

"Thanks."

"I can't even imagine what you must be going through right now."

"Yeah . . . it's been pretty surreal. It actually kind of felt like I was going crazy last night."

"I'll bet. Are you better now?"

"I think I'm a little saner today." Okay, that might be an over-statement, but no sense in worrying her too much.

"Well, I'll keep praying for you and your dad, too. I called the church prayer chain too, but someone there had already heard the news and they've been praying for you guys since yesterday."

"Oh . . ."

"I just can't believe the timing, Cleo. That the same day I move away, you find out your mom's been killed. That's just so weird."

"Yeah, it's been hard. I should probably go now," I say, even though I don't really need to. "There's a lot to do today." Another lie. Lie upon lie upon lie. If my lies were bricks, I might be able to build a house. Or a box. Or a prison cell.

"All right. But call me if I can do anything, *okay*? Even if it's just to listen. You know I'm a good listener, Cleo."

"Yeah, I know. Thanks." Then we say good-bye, and I turn off my phone. I really don't want to talk to anyone today. Not even Lola. And the reason I don't want to talk to Lola is because I'm not being completely honest with her. I didn't tell her how and why my mom died. Of course, she didn't ask. Not specifically anyway. But it would've been coming. And then what would I say? More lies? Or would I just try to avoid answering? And how is that different from outright lying?

It is a slow and steady torture knowing it's my fault my mother was murdered, but it would be even worse if I had to admit this to anyone. I cannot imagine how my dad would react if he knew the truth. Or Aunt Kellie. They both loved Mom, maybe as much as I did. How can I ever tell them, or anyone for that matter, that I am the reason she is dead? For now . . . and maybe forever . . . this will remain my deep, dark secret.

After "haunting" the house last night, I feel completely exhausted today. Drained. So I go back to bed. Sleep would be a welcome escape. As I close my eyes, I remember how my mother used to read fairy tales to me, and how much I loved the story about Sleeping Beauty. I'm not even sure why since the passive princess mostly just slept while the prince did all of the work to rescue her. Maybe it was because she looked so serenely beautiful in the illustration, peacefully sleeping as thorns grew over the castle.

As I feel myself drifting off, I wish I could sleep for days, weeks, months on end. Is it possible to lull oneself into a coma? I would like that.

· · · · · · · · · ·

"Cleo, Cleo . . . wake up. *Wake up*."

Still wrapped in thick slumber, I feel like I'm trying to emerge from a pudding-like fog, but I feel certain I can hear my mother's voice calling me. And I want to wake up. Yet when I open my eyes, it's not her. It's Aunt Kellie.

"You don't want to sleep your life away, honey."

I don't? I close my eyes and turn away, pulling my comforter tightly around me.

"Come on, Cleo. I know you're sad. We're all sad. But sleeping won't help." She peels my comforter away from me, and I sit up and glare at her.

"Just leave me alone," I snarl.

"That's not what your mom would want."

"How do you know what she'd want?"

"You know how much your mom loved you. It would break her heart to see you suffering like this."

"Mom is gone." I grab back my comforter.

"I know." She sits on the edge of my bed. "But you're still here, Cleo."

Tell me about it. "Please. Just leave me alone."

Now she stands and I think maybe she's going to go. But instead she bends over and starts making the trundle bed. I just watch her with narrowed eyes, thinking, *Fine, let her make that bed. And then she can get out of here.* But she doesn't stop there. The next thing I know she is straightening my room, acting as if I'm not even here, as if she hasn't totally invaded my space.

"Just leave that stuff alone," I tell her as she gathers up my dirty laundry.

"Your mom wouldn't want you living in squalor, Cleo."

"My mother isn't here!"

"But I am," she says calmly. "And since you seem unable to get up and clean your room, I will—"

"Get out of here!" I yell now. "I can clean my own room."

With one brow arched, she just looks at me.

"Go on!" I get out of bed and snatch the dirty clothes from her. "This is my room. I will take care of it."

She nods. "Okay then."

I stand there just glaring at her. I'm stunned at how much rage I feel toward my aunt. It's like she's the devil—and I hate her. I know it's totally irrational and it would make my mother sad to know this, but it's how I feel. And at the moment, my aunt and I are having a silent stare down, but I'm pretty sure I can win.

I give her my best snooty expression now. Holding my dirty laundry, I stand there with narrowed eyes, taking her inventory in exactly the way some of the snottiest girls at my school might do. And although I hate when that's done to me and I've never done it to anyone else, it's like I can't stop myself. Like something in me is terribly broken. And despite knowing it's wrong, I don't even care that I'm treating my aunt like this. I look at her like she's something smelly stuck to the bottom of my shoe.

But seriously, I've always wondered how this woman can possibly be a relative when she looks and smells like an alien from another planet. Planet Frumpy. Aunt Kellie is a few years younger than my mother, but I've always thought she looked much older. Prematurely gray and overweight, she's dowdy and homely and dresses like a bad advertisement for a ValueMart clearance rack. And yet she seems totally oblivious to her appearance. It's like she's completely clueless as to how pathetic she looks. Even when my mom used to take her shopping, trying to help her, Aunt Kellie resisted. I suppose she simply doesn't care.

It could be the result of not having a daughter, someone who could point out this woman's fashion faux pas. Because, seriously, I never would have allowed my mother to leave the house looking like *that*. But then Aunt Kellie never had kids. She married this old dude who is about twenty years older than her, and I'm pretty sure they sleep in separate beds. Not that it's any of my business, but I overheard my mother talking to her before. And it always sounded pretty sad. Anyway, to say my Aunt Kellie is a loser is not really an exaggeration.

Finally our stare-down comes to an end, and I assume my aunt has decided it's useless to reason with me. After she leaves my room, I firmly (as in hint-hint) slam my door. I wish I had a dead bolt. Maybe I'll get one if this woman continues to impose her presence upon us, which I'm sure is possible since she seems to think we need "looking after" as she puts it.

I throw my dirty clothes back onto the floor, give them a kick to splay them about in a messy way, then get back into bed. Aunt Kellie might be my mother's only sister, but that doesn't earn her the right to tell me what to do or how to live (rather *not* live) my life. And the sooner she figures this out, the better off we'll all be.

If I had more nerve—and who knows it might be just a matter of time—I would say, "Go home, Aunt Kellie. You are so not wanted here!"

## ···[CHAPTER 8]···············

On Monday, I refuse to go to school and no one questions this. Aunt Kellie defends me, saying I'm still "in mourning." Like maybe I should be wearing a black veil or something. Whatever. But by afternoon I am pacing around the house and feeling somewhat insane, not to mention sleep deprived since I was unable to sleep last night — and for some reason I can't sleep today either.

What if I'm unable to ever sleep again? What if the punishment for what I've done — my own personal hell — is to be forever awake and conscious of my guilt? My guilt that I can never, ever confess. My guilt that will have to accompany me to the grave.

At first, I'd been surprised that my dad hadn't questioned why my mom was in the city on Friday night. He never voiced any curiosity over what it was that put her "in the wrong place at the wrong time," as the police had said. But last night I heard Dad talking to Aunt Kellie. He was in his office and unaware I was listening. And really, I hadn't intended to eavesdrop, but I was sitting in the living room with the lights out and with his voice raised like that, I couldn't help but overhear.

"This is all due to that stupid bachelorette party," he ranted.

"If Karen hadn't gone to that idiotic bash, she would still be here right now."

"You can't blame a party for what happened to Karen," Aunt Kelly told him.

"I can if I want to! And why, pray tell, does a woman in her late fifties feel the need to have a *bachelorette* party in the first place? For Pete's sake, it was Trina's *third* wedding. She could've just quietly gotten married and let that be the end of it. But, no, she's got to plan some ridiculous shindig in the city, gathering all her old girlfriends around her like she thinks she's Sarah Jessica Parker. Then she keeps them out late at night, and I'm sure there was a lot of drinking going on, too."

"But Karen doesn't . . . I mean, didn't ever drink."

"No, that's just my point. Trina and her childishly selfish bachelorette party. Karen shouldn't have gone to it. She was *never* like that! It was Trina's bad influence—Trina is to blame for all of this!"

"Oh, Hugh. You're just hurting."

"You bet I'm hurting! Trina's partially responsible for Karen's death. If she hadn't insisted on having that senseless party, my wife would still be alive today. Can you deny that, Kellie?"

"It's not fair to blame Trina. She never—"

"It's not fair that I have lost my wife! In fact, after she gets back from her honeymoon, I've got a mind to call up Trina and tell her just that."

"Oh, Hugh!" Aunt Kellie switches to a scolding tone now. "You wouldn't dare. Really, how would that make Karen feel?"

"She can't feel anything, Kellie. She is dead."

"Karen is not dead. She is alive with God in heaven. You know she was a believer, Hugh. How can you talk like that?"

"Maybe I should blame God then," my dad challenged her.

"Why did he let my wife die a horrible death like that? Why?"

"God doesn't control people. If humans make wrong choices, like to murder someone, God doesn't stop them."

"So you're saying God let Karen be killed? And I should blame him?"

"That's not what I'm saying, Hugh."

"Are you saying God couldn't have prevented Karen's death? He's not big enough or strong enough to keep some druggie thug from killing my wife? Because if that's right, I have no respect for a God like that."

"I'm not saying that either." Aunt Kellie sounded frustrated. "I'm just saying you can't keep blaming others for Karen's death."

"What then? Should I blame myself? That I shouldn't have been traveling? That I could've prevented it if I'd been home?"

"It's just your pain talking right now. You're not rational. In time you'll see that trying to blame someone else, or even your-self, is a perfectly natural part of the grieving process. You want to make sense of what feels like madness. You want to blame something or someone for your loss."

"And Trina Billings is an easy target," he snapped. "I'll blame her!"

"The only one you can honestly blame for Karen's death is the murderer, Hugh. He's the one who committed such a sense-less crime. If you need to blame someone, why not blame him?"

There was a long silence after that. Finally my dad spoke in a hoarse voice. "I know . . . I know . . ." And then he broke into loud sobs. The sound of my father crying like that sliced through me like a dull, rusty knife. I couldn't bear to hear it. And I rushed to my bedroom, closed the door, and wrapped my pillow around my head, covering my ears until I was sure it was over with.

Even after the house finally got quiet, I still couldn't sleep. By midnight, I was playing Ghost Girl again, wandering throughout the house, wishing and wishing I could undo everything . . . or somehow fix this mess. But that's impossible.

Even if I stepped up and told my dad exactly who is to blame for my mother's death—not Trina, not him . . . *but me*—I don't think it would help our situation. He wouldn't be relieved to hear my confession. In fact, I suspect he would be outraged, so angry that I had lied and disobeyed, that he would probably disown me. Honestly, after hearing him go on and on about Trina, I don't see how he could ever forgive me. And who would blame him for that?

I can't tell him. He's already lost his wife. How could I be so cruel as to force him to lose his daughter as well? And yet, it seems he already has. I feel like I've destroyed our family. Like all this pain is my fault . . . and it will always be my burden to bear. But what if it's too heavy?

More than anything I long for an escape, a way to stop the never-ending pain gnawing away at my insides. I feel desperate and frantic . . . like I'm holding on by a frazzled thread. Lola has called and left several sweet messages, but I'm afraid to return her calls. Afraid that I'll let the truth slip out, the real reason my mom died. I have to push Lola away from me now. It's too risky to be friends anymore. As hard as it is, it's a good thing she lives so far away.

A little before two o'clock, Dad and Aunt Kellie are about to leave for the mortuary to make the arrangements for my mother's funeral. I opt out of this appointment, and neither of them questions me. Instead they look at me with sympathetic eyes, as if I'm the biggest victim in this pool of pain. They do not suspect that I am nearly as guilty as the murderer, maybe even more so since the murderer didn't specifically choose my mother to kill and rob. He probably just went for the easiest target. I was the one who set my mother up for him.

Knowing I'm alone in the house for a while, I go into the master bedroom and into the walk-in closet my parents shared. I stand amid my mother's clothes, inhaling the aroma that still smells like her. It's a clean mix of her favorite perfume, Miracle, and the smell of freshly pressed clothes and something else, something indescribable, something that is simply the essence of her.

But the smell of that perfume, a spicy floral blend, gives me an idea. I slip into their bathroom, and there on the counter is the rectangular pink bottle. I pick it up and almost spray some, but my dad might come in here and smell it . . . and that would probably just depress him even more. Instead I remove the lid and take a quick sniff, and I'm immediately transported to the day she and I found this particular fragrance.

We were clothes shopping for me, the summer before I started high school, and it was the first time my mom had been out after having knee surgery. We stopped by the perfume counter so she could sit and rest for a bit. That was when I urged her to try out some new perfumes. I wanted her to get something for herself since, as usual, she'd been focused on me. And when she smelled this Lancôme fragrance, she instantly liked it, so I talked her into splurging.

"It smells so good that I'm almost light-headed," she admitted as she squirted herself again. "I think it might be more effective than my pain pills—and cheaper too." The salesgirl and I laughed at that, but my mother bought the perfume and it became her signature fragrance.

I take another whiff now, wishing that my mother's Miracle

perfume would miraculously take away my pain and make me light-headed too. But instead it makes me feel like I'm going to sneeze. I wipe my nose with a tissue. Knowing full well that I'm way out of line, I open my parents' medicine cabinet and stare at the myriad items stored there. Might there possibly be something here to take away my pain?

I pick up a brown prescription bottle, but it's for my dad's allergies. I put it back, in the exact same spot. But as I dig a bit deeper I find that, just as I suspected, my mom's old prescription for Vicodin is still here. I open it to discover that the bottle is about half full. I pour all but a few of the pills into a tissue, then wrap them up and pocket the bundle, returning the nearly empty bottle back to the exact same spot.

My hands are shaking and my heart is pounding as I hurry to the hall bathroom and pop a pill into my mouth, washing it down with lukewarm tap water. I stand there looking in the mirror, waiting for it to take effect. I know this is wrong. And yet I know that everything else about my life is even more wrong. So somehow, this wrong doesn't really seem to matter as much.

As I stare at the image of the girl in the mirror, I am certain she is a stranger. The long blonde hair that needs washing is dull and lifeless. The complexion looks pasty, the lips pale, the only noticeable contrast is the smudgy shadows beneath the dark holes that must be my eyes—eyes my mother used to say were dark chocolate. But it's the expression in those eyes that gets me. So lost . . . empty . . . dead.

I'm not sure how long I stand there, but after a while I think I feel something happening. At first it's a little bit tingly and then, just as my mother described, I feel a little light-headed. And to my complete surprise, that feels good. It's like a bit of the weight has been lifted from me. Perhaps the edge has been taken off that deep pain. Whatever it is, I like it. My mother's pills are working. And I almost wonder if she left them behind on purpose . . . to help me through this difficult time. At least that's what I'm telling myself.

· · · · · · · ·

On Wednesday morning, and about a dozen Vicodin pills later, I am able to shower and wash my hair in preparation for my mother's funeral. I wear a navy blue dress that my mother always liked on me, but I don't bother to blow dry my hair, knowing full well it will end up wavy not straight. But I don't really care about my looks. Why should I?

I've been informed that the service is "closed casket," but on the way to the church, my dad informs me that we are going early for a family viewing time.

"Family viewing time?" I frown.

"So you can pay your last respects to your mother," Aunt Kellie tells me. "To see her one last time."

"Your aunt thought it was a good idea."

"You want me to stand in front of the coffin of my dead mother and look at her?"

"You don't have to," Dad quickly tells me.

"But it might be healthy for you—"

"There is no way I'm doing that," I cut her off. "That's just morbid."

"No one is going to make you," Dad assures me. "We just thought you might want—"

"Well, please, don't do my thinking for me. I would much rather remember Mom how she was."

Dad just nods, driving silently toward the church. They go inside, but I wait in the car. After a while the sunlight makes the car too warm. So I get out and just walk around. I already took one pill a couple of hours ago, but I had a feeling that wouldn't cut it, so I tucked two precious pills into my pocket. Already I'm getting concerned that my stockpile is shrinking. But mostly I just want to make it through this day . . . as painlessly as possible.

Other cars start to pull into the parking lot, and I assume that means "family viewing time" will be coming to an end and perhaps it's safe to go in.

But on my way, I stop by the drinking fountain and discreetly take one of my backup pills. All I want is to numb the pain and get this thing over with. I go into the sanctuary, where a few seats are starting to fill, and I spot my dad sitting with Aunt Kellie and Uncle Don and a few other relatives up in front.

Feeling like I'm not completely here or like maybe I'm just a player on a stage, I walk up the aisle and take a seat by my dad. He reaches over and takes my hand, giving me what I'm sure is supposed to be a comforting squeeze. I squeeze back but feel like Judas when he kissed Jesus. Then I pull my hand back and, folding my hands and putting them in my lap like I'm five years old, look straight ahead. Flowers are everywhere—lots of pinks and purples—and I suspect that Aunt Kellie tipped off the florist as to my mother's favorite colors.

Now my eyes come to rest on the casket. It is a light-colored wood with brass trim. I have no idea who picked it out or why, but for some reason I think my mother would not have approved. She preferred dark woods. Then, in the midst of my critique over these superficial things, it hits me—my mother is inside that box! She is dead. Murdered while on a mission to rescue me, she is never coming back. And it is my fault.

I look down at my lap now, feeling tears rolling down my cheeks, watching them drop into my lap, making dark wet spots on the skirt of my blue dress.

"Here, honey." Aunt Kellie slips me a couple of tissues.

I just nod, mumbling thanks, keeping my eyes down as I wipe my cheeks and blow my nose. All I can think is, *When is that extra pill going to kick in? When will the pain go away? Or at least lessen?* Finally, after a woman named Fiona sings a couple of songs, the pastor steps up to the podium. Just as he begins to speak, I start feeling a little dizzy and light-headed, but I don't mind. I just hope I don't pass out.

To keep myself from falling asleep, I focus on Pastor Reynolds's mustache as it moves up and down, and I count every time he uses the word *she*. I'm clear up to seventeen by the time he ends his little speech, but at least I'm still awake. Then a few more songs are sung, one of the elders prays, and it's over.

As we're ushered out, I'm surprised at how many people are packed into our church's sanctuary. Dad and my aunt and I form a reception line for those who want to walk by and express their regrets, et cetera, and I'm even more surprised at how many of these people claim to have dearly loved my mother. Many speak as if my mom was their closest friend, and one woman tells me that with my mom gone, there will be a big hole in her life. Maybe my mom really was friends with all these people, but she sure could've fooled me. I always assumed I was the only person she cared that much about, the one she invested herself into . . . and that besides Dad and me, she had no life. Maybe I was wrong.

It's a lot to take in, and it's not easy acting like I'm really here when I keep fading in and out and things get a little fuzzy. But it doesn't escape my attention that a lot of kids from my school are here. Some are ones I know and some are ones who've never said a word to me. Since the funeral started at ten, they must've been excused from classes to come today. Maybe that's the reason they're here — a get-out-of-school-for-free card.

Even so, I try to act civilized and gracious to all of them, even to a girl named Brittany, whose most common nickname starts with the same letter as her first name. But I thank her for coming. And I try to remain clear and focused, which is a huge challenge considering how my head is floating way up high near the rafters just now.

"How are you holding up, Cleo?" Daniel Crane asks me as he moves along with the other well-wishers. He's one of the last people in line, and I can tell he's a little uncomfortable about being here.

I spied him earlier, but I still can't believe he's actually here or that he knows my name. I've been secretly infatuated with this guy since sophomore year when his family moved to town and he started coming to our youth group for a while. Anyway, he's never actually spoken to me before, and eventually he faded out of youth group. I'm guessing because his life got too busy since he somehow made it into the popular crowd at school. Partly due, I'm sure, to his good looks and because he's a nice guy, but also because he's a natural athlete. This year he was elected as senior class president, so it's hard to believe he's actually talking to me. I suddenly realize I should respond.

"It's been pretty hard," I finally say.

"I'm sure it's even harder with Lola gone," he says with unexpected understanding.

I blink. "You knew Lola?"

"Sure. She came to this church, too. And it was obvious you

two were really close friends."

I nod as a lump grows in my throat. "Yeah, I miss Lola a lot. But at least she's not gone for good. I mean . . . you know . . . like my mom."

"I was really devastated when my grandpa died last fall. He and I had been pretty close. But I can't imagine how hard it would be to lose a parent . . . and so tragically." He puts his hand on my shoulder, giving it a gentle squeeze that sends a warm shiver down my back. "If you ever need someone to talk to, Cleo . . . well, I'm a good listener."

I want to ask him if he's serious, but I can tell by his eyes, which are kind of a blue-green color, he means this. And I'm totally taken aback. "Thanks," I tell him as my dad motions to me, hinting that it's time to go to the cemetery. "It would be good to have someone to talk to . . . at school."

"Then I expect you to take me up on that offer."

"Thanks. I appreciate it."

Soon we are riding in the back of the limo to the cemetery—Dad and me and Aunt Kellie and Uncle Don. No one speaks as our car follows the slate-gray hearse. We move through town at a snail's pace, inching our way up to the cemetery. I stare blankly out the window, seeing the same buildings and businesses I have seen for my whole life, but now they look unfamiliar. Even as our procession passes by Madame Reginald's Ballet Academy, I feel as if I've never been inside that brick building. As if my mother had never taken me for a single lesson there.

I close my eyes, trying to block out everything. To my relief that pleasant buzzy-dizzy feeling returns, softening the sharp, harsh edges of my shattered life. But my relief is hindered by nagging concerns. I wonder how long it will be until I need to take another pill . . . and if I should've brought more with me . . . and what will I do when I run out? But thankfully, this pill is doing its magic. I forget where I am, feeling as if I'm wrapped in a thick, fuzzy blanket.

Then, just like that, the lulling ride comes to a halt. Doors open, loudly close, people are speaking to me, but I can't understand their words. Or maybe this is a dream. I look around, trying to absorb my surroundings, wondering where I am.

"Come on, Cleo." With sad eyes, my dad reaches for my hand, helping me out of the car.

And that's when I realize we're in the cemetery. And like a glass of icy water that's been thrown in my face, I remember why we're here.

We follow the men in dark suits as they transport the casket across the cemetery. The grass is damp, and my feet soon become soggy as we trudge up a hill. I vaguely remember these men—are they called pallbearers, and if so what does that mean? I'm pretty sure they are from our church, but I can't even think of their names. How did they come to be doing this depressing task? Did my dad call them up and ask them to carry his wife like this? Will they also help to bury her?

I wish I could take the other pill now. Something to stop this flow of thoughts . . . something to block my brain. But now we are being seated in a row of folding chairs directly across from where the casket is now arranged over the hole—the hole that will swallow my mother. I close my eyes and wish I could join her. Better yet, I wish I could trade places. So much simpler.

Again, the words being spoken seem to float over my head. And when it's time to stand, to sing "Amazing Grace," I get a rush of dizziness, followed by a loud buzzing in my ears that won't go away . . . and then darkness.

When I come to, my aunt is looking at my face. "There you are," she says in that despicable congenial tone she likes to use.

"See, Hugh, she's simply fainted. I knew she should've eaten breakfast."

"I — I'm sorry." I sit up from where I was laid out on the row of folding chairs. Looking around, I'm relieved to see that the graveside service seems to be over; people are leaving. Before long, only our immediate family and Pastor Reynolds remain behind. My dad is standing by the casket. As he lays a single red rose on top, I look away.

"Come on now." Aunt Kellie reaches for my hand. "Let's get you back into the car." Then with Uncle Don and Aunt Kellie flanking me on both sides, holding on to my arms like I might topple over again, we go back to the limo, where I lean back into the seat, closing my eyes, longing for an escape as my aunt lectures me about low blood sugar. She tries to get me to eat a peppermint, which I can't stand, but to placate her, I do.

Finally my dad joins us, and once again, we are on our way. Will this day never end?

"That was a very nice service, Hugh." Aunt Kellie makes this sweeping statement like we're simply on our way home from church — not from burying a loved one.

"Yes . . ." Dad sighs. "It seemed to go well." But he peers curiously at me now. "Except for that little fainting bit. Cleo?"

"What?"

"Are you okay?"

"Aunt Kellie said I had low blood sugar." I look away, wondering if he suspects that I've been sneaking my mother's old pain pills. But that's absurd. How could he possibly know?

When we arrive at home, it smells like a bad buffet and is crawling with people. All I want to do is escape to my room and crash, but before I get the chance, Aunt Kellie corners me in the kitchen, insisting I need to eat something.

"But I'm not hungry."

"You don't *feel* hungry," she tells me, "but you still need to eat."

"And you need to visit with our guests." My dad drops some used paper plates into a grocery bag that's doubling as a garbage container by the back door.

Aunt Kellie nods in agreement. "Your dad is right, Cleo. It's your job to play hostess today. Your mom would expect that much of you."

So I eat some bites of a casserole that tastes like a combination of processed cheese and sawdust. I top that off with a piece of chocolate cake that's so sweet it makes my teeth hurt. Then I ask to be excused for a few minutes. "Just to use the bathroom," I explain as I take a can of soda from the ice chest.

"Of course," Aunt Kellie says sweetly. "Just don't forget to come back."

I head to the hall bathroom, which is actually in use, so instead I go to my parents' bathroom where I take my other pill, washing it down with soda. Then flushing the toilet for effect, I open their medicine cabinet, looking to see if the bottle of Vicodin is still where I left it. It seems to be in the same place. I empty the remaining pills into a tissue, which I wrap up like a minipackage, then slip into my bra. But before I leave, I pour a couple dozen aspirin tablets into the empty Vicodin bottle. Just in case my dad should check.

Then I go out, trying to play the role of "hostess," but everyone keeps talking about my mom, saying what a generous and kind person she was, how it was too soon to lose her . . . on and on. And I have no response to that.

"Your mother was an absolute saint," a woman named Maria tells me. "Do you know how she helped me when Julio was born?"

I blink, trying to focus on this woman's amazing eyes — they are black and shiny as glass. "No . . . I don't recall."

"She was an angel. Three years ago, I was pregnant with Julio and my husband had left me with nothing. Your mother arranged a baby shower at church, and she helped me to find furniture at secondhand shops and . . ." On she goes, but the words are like colorful balloons floating off into the nethersphere, over my head and far out of my reach.

"And sh-she helped find me a place to live," a middle-aged man with a serious lisp and stammer tells me. He seems to know Maria and I think I've seen him at church before, but I can't remember his name. "I was homeless-ss and jobless-ss." Like an impaired snake, he gets stuck on the *s* sound, but he nods over and over for emphasis. "That was about ss-six years ago. I've been working ever ss-since."

Feeling like a bobblehead doll, I mimic his nod. "That's great. I'm so happy for you."

Maria continues talking about Julio and how much he loved "Aunt Karen" and how she sometimes babysat him. "Right here in this house." She looks around with a sad smile.

"Right here?" I glance about the family room, trying to imagine my mother caring for a toddler . . . and me not even knowing.

As Maria and the lisp man continue to recall my mother's attributes, I feel dizzy and spacey and I need to lie down. "I'm sorry," I interrupt Maria. "But I'm not feeling too well."

"Oh yes." She puts her hand on my shoulder. "I forget how hard this must be for you."

I nod again, and this time the mere motion of moving my head makes me feel like the walls are spinning . . . like I'm about to throw up. So I excuse myself and, trying to get my bearings, hurry from that stuffy room, rushing down the hallway toward my bedroom. But I feel like a rat in a maze, like I'm lost and can't find the right turn . . . until finally, I find the right door, go inside, close it, then fall onto my bed . . . and escape into a foggy darkness.

When I wake, my dad is sitting on the side of my bed. His expression is one of great concern and sadness. "What's wrong with you, Cleo?"

I sit up and blink at the overhead light. "Huh?"

"Are you sick? Do you need to see a doctor?"

I shrug, then let out a long sigh. "I'm just really sad. And tired."

"I know . . ." He nods. "Believe me, I know. But we can't give up. We have to keep going. That's what your mom would want us to do."

I look down at my hands, thinking they look like someone else's hands. My mom's perhaps?

"But if you can't keep going . . ." Dad reaches over and takes one of my hands in his. "Then we will get you help."

"Help?"

"Someone to help you through your grief. Aunt Kellie said she knows someone who —"

"I don't need someone to help me," I say stubbornly. Then I pull my hand away from his and slide my feet out from under the blanket and onto the floor. "I can deal with this myself."

"I know it's not easy. But we have to get through this, Cleo."

"I know, Dad." I stand up now, feeling both shaky and dizzy . . . and like I need another pain pill. "I'm getting through it the best way I can. I just need time."

"Okay, I know it's going to take time." He rubs his hand through his messy hair. "And I hate to tell you this, but I'm scheduled to go to Denver next week. I thought about canceling, but we need the—"

"Don't cancel for my sake."

"But I hate to think of leaving you here . . . alone . . . after what's happened."

"I'll be okay. I know you have to keep working, Dad."

"If I wasn't self-employed, I could take time off, but being my own boss . . . if I cancel on a client . . . well, you know how it goes."

"I understand, Dad. It's okay for you to work. I'll be fine."

"Well, my flight isn't until Sunday evening. I can always cancel—"

"No," I say firmly. "You don't need to cancel." I stand a bit straighter now, trying to convey confidence. "In fact, I plan to return to school tomorrow."

He looks relieved. "Oh, good. I think it will be good to get back to our old lives."

I glance over my dad's shoulder. "Does that mean Aunt Kellie went home?"

He makes an uncomfortable frown. "Not yet."

"Why not?"

He shrugs. "I think she's worried about you, Cleo."

"I'm fine."

"Well, you might have to convince her of that." He moves toward the door. "In the meantime, she's not budging. She just told me that your mother wants her here."

"What?" I ask hotly. "Is she able to speak to the dead?"

My dad says nothing, but his expression says it all. Sad, weary, lost. And it's all my fault. Unable to see so much sorrow in my dad, I turn away from him, pretending to be busy with a tangled necklace on my dresser.

"Kellie said to tell you she's putting out some leftovers for dinner."

"Dinner?" I scowl. "Didn't we just have lunch?"

"It's almost seven," he says as he leaves my room.

I look at the clock by my bed. It *is* almost seven. I have been asleep for nearly six hours. Six hours of blissful escape. I close my door, then go to my secret stash of pills. I've been very creative. I wrapped them in a tube of tissue that is stuffed into a cardboard tampon container, and this is wrapped in the plastic and stuck in the box, looking just like the others. In fact, it takes me a few seconds to figure out which one it is.

Then I remove the pills I stuffed in my bra and put them with this stash. But not before I take one more pill. I need another pill to make it through this night. Tomorrow I will try to begin weaning myself from the pills . . . or at least slow it down.

A half hour later, as we're finishing up dinner, which I pretend to eat for my aunt's sake, my dad mentions that he's heard from the police. "They called this afternoon," he says as I'm returning some of the food dishes to the kitchen.

"Karen's car turned up," he says in a flat tone.

"Really?" Aunt Kellie is still sitting at the table. "What kind of shape is it in?"

"I don't know. Apparently it still runs."

"Does that mean you'll be getting it back soon?" she asks him.

"Not until after they collect their evidence." Dad's voice is grim. "That might take a week or so."

"Then perhaps Cleo can have it to use," Aunt Kellie suggests.

I come back into the dining room, surprised but not saying anything.

Dad clears his throat. "Oh, I don't think so."

"Why not?" I ask him. "As it is, I don't have a way to get to school now that Lola's moved. Well, unless I ride the school bus, which is pretty humiliating at my age. I wouldn't mind having Mom's car."

"It's a bad idea, Cleo." Dad sets his water glass down with a thud.

"I don't see why." Aunt Kellie is stacking our plates now. "I think Karen would be happy to have Cleo using her car."

"It doesn't seem right." My dad scoots back his chair with a loud scraping sound of wood on wood.

"You don't have to drive it," I tell him.

He just shakes his head as he stands. "Fine. If you really want a car—a car that—well, *you know*. If you want to drive *that* car, you're welcome to it." Then he walks away.

I look at Aunt Kellie with uncertainty. "Maybe it's not such a good idea . . ."

"Oh, don't be silly, Cleo. Your mother loved that car. And she loved you. No reason you shouldn't get to use it. It makes perfect sense."

I bite my lip, trying to imagine how it will feel to drive the car that my mom spent some of her last living moments in. Maybe I don't want it after all.

"Anyway, you don't have to think about that now," she tells me.

"But I do need a way to get to school tomorrow."

"I plan to drive you there."

"Oh . . ." I just nod. "Thanks."

"And I'll pick you up afterward for ballet. You still have it on Thursday afternoons, right?"

I frown. "Yes, but I don't think I want to go."

"Nonsense. Of course you're going to ballet. Isn't it nearly recital time? And your mother told me you're dancing the lead this year. Surely, you can't be skipping out on lessons now."

"But I don't want to —"

"You can't quit living your life, Cleo. I know you're sad about your mom. We're all sad. But the best way to get over this is to move on — keep on doing what you need to do. That's what your mother would want."

She continues to ramble on about how proud my mother would be of me, how she'll probably be watching me doing things like ballet . . . graduation . . . getting married . . . having children . . . all from her luxurious front-row seat up in heaven, where she will be cheering me on as my biggest fan.

It's fine and good that Aunt Kellie can believe that if she wants to. I'd rather not think about it. Because *if* my mother can really see me from heaven, that means she must be fully aware I'm the one to blame for her death. Because of me, she went to the wrong place at the wrong time. I am the reason her life was cut short. I can hardly imagine her up there cheering about something like that.

**B**y Thursday morning, I know I need to ration my pills. At the rate I've been taking them, I'm down to two days' worth. But I figure if these pills can get me through the next couple of days . . . well, it's worth it.

"We better get going," Aunt Kellie tells me as soon as I emerge from the bathroom, where I've just taken my first pill of the day. "You don't want to be late."

"Don't I?" I bend down to put on my shoes.

"And do you have your ballet things with you for after school?"

I roll my eyes at her. "I already told you I'm not going anymore."

She looks wounded. "But you have to go to ballet, Cleo. What would your mother say if she knew you wanted to quit dancing?"

"*If?*" I frown at her. "I thought you said she was up there watching every move I make. Doesn't she know already?"

Now my aunt is flustered. She jingles her car keys in one hand and rubs her forehead with the other. "But you *love* ballet. And I've heard that dancing is very therapeutic."

"*Therapeutic?*"

"Yes, I saw something on *Good Morning America* about these kids who were having serious—"

"Really? *Good Morning America*? How impressive," I say sarcastically.

"Yes, well, their point was that dancing helped them to forget their problems and it was very—"

"Maybe *you'd* like to take up ballet," I say in a snooty tone. I really don't like being this way, but it's like I can't help myself.

She just laughs. "Oh yes, imagine *me* in a tutu."

"*Imagine.*" I pick up my bag, looping a strap over my shoulder. "I'm ready to go now."

Aunt Kellie keeps chattering away, going on about ballet and how wonderful it is, as she drives me to school. As much as I appreciate the ride, I'm suddenly aware of how embarrassing her car is. It's not only dirty, both inside and out, but it's a *minivan.*

"Why do you drive this anyway?"

"What?" She seems confused.

"This minivan. Why do you drive it?"

"Why not?" She smiles obliviously.

"Well, because I thought they were for people with little kids."

"I suppose so. I just happen to like it. It feels safe, and it's big enough to haul things in."

"Right . . ." I hate myself. I really do. Why am I such a witch?

"Here you go." She pulls up in front of the school.

"Thanks," I mutter as I open the door.

"See you at three," she calls out.

"Yeah." I nod, hurrying away from the minivan, but not fast enough to avoid some curious stares. Like why's a senior arriving at school in a minivan? But that actually seems minor compared to my realization that this is the first time I've come to school without the comfort of Lola by my side. I can't believe how much I miss her. And yet I've been avoiding her calls. Or when I do answer, I just cut things short, saying I'm too busy to talk, or else I lie to her. Like I'm shoving her away with both hands. It's like I've turned into someone else.

To my relief, the pain pill begins to take effect as I go into my first class. That fuzzy, blurry feeling returns; slowly it dulls the sharp, jagged edges of my life. But by second period, I can't really focus. I lean my head forward, resting it on my bag. I close my eyes, and everything just slips away. I wake to the sound of a bell, and then I look up to see Mr. Jones looking at me.

"Are you okay, Cleo?" His eyes are concerned.

"I . . . uh . . . yeah. I was just tired. Sorry."

He continues looking at me, peering closely as if trying to see deep into my soul. "I was very sorry to hear about your mother. You have my deepest sympathy."

"Thanks," I murmur as I gather my things and stand.

"Would you do me a favor?"

I frown, wondering why a teacher wants a favor from me.

"Would you go talk to Mrs. Stanley?"

"The counselor?"

He nods. "I think it would be good to tell her how you're feeling."

"Why?"

He shrugs. "Just a feeling I have, that you might need some help with this. It's a lot to deal with, Cleo."

I don't say anything.

"Just go see Mrs. Stanley, okay? She's a very understanding person. You can tell her anything."

"Okay," I say reluctantly. "I'll go."

He smiles. "Thanks. I don't think you'll regret it."

I just shake my head. "If you say so." I make my way out as the next class is coming in. But as I'm going through the doorway, I come face-to-face with Daniel Crane.

"Cleo," he says with a smile. "How are you doing?"

I shrug. "I've had better days."

"Anything I can do for you?"

"Not at the moment." I tip my head toward Mr. Jones. "I'm being sent to Mrs. Stanley . . . to talk."

Daniel nods in a thoughtful way. "That's probably a good thing. Mrs. Stanley is great. I've talked to her before myself."

"Really?" Now this surprises me.

"Yeah. She's cool."

"Okay."

He pats me on the back. "See you around then?"

"Yeah . . . sure."

As I walk toward the guidance center, the tardy bell for third period rings, but I figure I'll get excused anyway. I tell the receptionist who I am and what Mr. Jones asked me to do.

"Oh, you're the one . . . the girl whose mother . . ." She sighs sadly. "I'm so sorry for your loss, Cleo."

"Thanks." I twist the handle of my bag. What good could possibly come from speaking to a counselor? It's not like I'm going to tell her the truth.

"Have a seat and I'll check with Mrs. Stanley."

I go over to the couch and just sit there, but I feel like I'm about to fall asleep again. I blink several times, trying to wake myself up. And then a tall, dark-haired woman is looking down at me. "Cleo?" she says gently.

I nod, trying to focus in on her face. I think she's pretty, but

I nod, tears stinging my eyes. "That makes sense, too."

"The third stage is anger and bargaining. This is when you lash out at people around you . . . maybe you blame someone else for your mother's death . . . maybe you blame your-self—that's linked to the guilt. But it's perfectly normal to feel this kind of anger. And it's best to let it out. And then bargaining is our way of trying to regain control over a situation beyond our control." She smiles sadly. "But we do it anyway. I was in my early twenties when my father died, and I told God I'd quit smoking if he'd bring my dad back."

I just nod. "I've already tried to bargain, too." I don't admit that I've asked God to trade my life for my mother's. That would require too much explaining.

"The good part was that I did quit smoking." She sighs. "Of course, it didn't bring my dad back. But I'm sure he'd be happy to know I quit." Now she goes over the fourth stage, which is depression. She explains that this is when you push people away from you and how it can be very lonely. "This is when it's help-ful to be in a grief group," she tells me. Then she goes over the next three stages—the upward turn, reconstruction, and accep-tance and hope. It all sounds reassuring . . . for someone else, that is.

"So what stage do you think you're at?"

I study the brochure. "I don't know. I can relate to a lot of the things in the first four stages."

"That's perfectly normal, too. You can bounce from stage one to stage three and then go to stage two. The good thing is to understand that this is simply how people feel when they lose someone. If you know what to expect, such as that you'll be unreasonably angry at times, it's comforting to know it's just normal. Or, say, if your father gets angry over something

irrational, you can remind yourself that he's probably just grieving, too. You know what I mean?"

"Yeah." I put the brochure in my bag. "I think that's going
to be helpful."

She smiles. "Good. Knowledge is power, you know?"

"Thanks for telling me about this." I want to go now. I don't
want to seem rude or ungrateful, but I don't want to talk to her
too long. I'm afraid I'll say too much.

"You're going to be okay, Cleo. But it's going to take time.
And you'll probably keep bouncing around in these first few
stages for a while. But I'm here for you . . . if you ever need to
talk. And I'd like to contact a grief group for you. I do think
that would be helpful." She makes a note of this. "I'll let you
know, okay?"

"Okay." I stand, thinking this is a good time to go. "I do
appreciate you talking to me."

She reaches out to shake my hand. "And I mean it, Cleo,
anytime you need to talk, just come on in to the guidance center.
If I'm with someone else, Ms. Farrell will make you an appointment. Okay?"

I nod. "Sounds good."

"Don't forget to ask Ms. Farrell for a hall pass."

"Right."

"Hang in there."

"Oh, yeah." I try to insert a bit of enthusiasm into my voice,
but it sounds false to my ears.

I make it to fourth period, art class, about ten minutes late.
Mrs. Lloyd gives me a hug, telling me how sorry she is for my
loss. I thank her, then get my current project out of my locker
and take a seat in the back of the room. I try to focus on the
acrylic painting, but my vision grows blurry so the cottage and

flower garden I was painting for my mom's Mother's Day gift is wrapped in thick fog.

"Hey, Cleo," Drew Mackey says to me. "Sorry to hear about your mom."

I thank him. Drew is kind of a character—artistic and unique. He has dreadlocks that go midway down his back. For years Lola has been pretty sure he's into drugs, but I've always defended him as a free spirit. And he's a good artist, too.

"Mind if I sit with you?" he asks.

"Sure, if you want. I'm not very good company."

"It's like a double bummer. You lose your mom like that and Lola moves away—all in the same weekend. Seriously, that is so twisted."

I nod. "Yeah."

"And the thing with your mom. Man, it's just so random . . . so unfair. What is wrong with the universe?"

I bite my lip.

"So, really, are you doing okay?" He's peering into my eyes with what seems like genuine concern.

"Not so good."

He nods. "Life is tough sometimes."

I suddenly get an idea. Studying him closely, I wonder if I'm completely losing my mind, or if I'm just really desperate. "Drew?" I say quietly, glancing around to be sure no one can hear me. "I . . . uh . . . I've been taking some of my mom's old pain pills." I blink back tears. "And they kind of help me through this. You know what I mean?"

"Oh yeah. Totally."

I look down at my painting again. What had started out so cheerful and bright now seems so garish, so wrong. Like me. I feel so ashamed. What am I doing?

"I know someone who can help you with that," he says in a hushed tone.

I look up in surprise. "You do?"

"Yeah. A friend of mine. T. J. He can help you."

My heart is pounding. What am I doing here? Am I actually initiating some kind of drug deal? How did I get to this place? But even as these thoughts are racing through my head, I watch as he tears off a piece of sketch paper. He writes down a phone number, then slides it over to me.

"T. J.'s a good guy. You can trust him, Cleo."

I slip the paper into my bag. "Thanks," I murmur as I stare at my painting.

I won't be using that phone number. I won't be calling this T. J. person. Good grief! That would be so incredibly stupid. Even more stupid than what I've already done. I will simply stop taking those pills. I can do it.

## CHAPTER 11

After school, Daniel joins me by the front entrance. "So . . . how did it go today? Your first day back at school? You doing okay?"

I attempt a forced smile. "I guess it went as well as it could go."

"How was Mrs. Stanley?"

I almost forgot I told him about that. "She was nice . . . helpful."

"Are you interested in getting coffee?"

I blink, trying to grasp what he's saying. "With you?"

He laughs uncomfortably. "Yeah, that's what I meant."

"Sure." I nod. "That would be—"

"Hey, Cleo!"

I look over to the street and see that white minivan, even dustier looking than this morning. Did she take it on a dirt road? And Aunt Kellie, wearing one of her horrible ValueMart outfits, is standing next to the minivan, waving wildly at me. "Time for ballet lessons!" she calls out like she wants the whole school to know.

Blood rushes to my cheeks as I turn back to Daniel, but he just smiles. "Looks like you have a previous engagement."

"Just ballet. And I told her I'm not going."

"I think it's cool that you do ballet, Cleo."

I frown. "Seriously?"

"Yeah. I'd love to see you dance."

"Come on, Cleo," my aunt yells. "You don't want to be late."

"How about you give me a rain check for coffee?" Daniel offers.

"Sure." I nod eagerly. "I'd like that."

"What time does your ballet class end?"

"Five."

"How about if I pick you up?"

"Really? That would be great."

"I'll bet you take lessons at Madame Reginald's Ballet Academy."

"How did you know that?"

"It's a small town, Cleo." He smiles and his eyes sparkle like sunlight on the ocean. "And my little sister used to take lessons there."

My aunt yells again.

"So I'll see you at five?" I say as I step away from him.

"I'll be there."

Feeling unreal, I jog over to the minivan and climb in. "I told you I didn't want to go to ballet today."

Aunt Kellie puts the van in gear. "I know what you said. But I didn't think you meant it."

"But I didn't bring my things and—"

"I found your ballet bag." She jerks her thumb toward the backseat. "I assumed your things were in it."

"Thanks a lot," I grumble.

"Who was that handsome young man you were talking to?" she asks with way too much curiosity.

"A friend."

"Oh . . . ?"

"Yes. A friend, Aunt Kellie. *Just* a friend."

As I'm getting out of the van in front of the ballet studio, I turn to my aunt. "By the way, my *friend* Daniel will pick me up after ballet so you don't need to get me."

"I don't mind picking you up."

I'm tempted to tell Aunt Kellie to get a life, but I remember the last time I said that. "Thanks," I tell her in a curt tone. "But I don't need you to. Okay?"

She nods.

I feel trapped as I go up the stairs. I do not want to dance today. I don't think I even remember how to dance. How does one dance with a bag of rocks tied to one's back? Feeling like a robot, or a zombie that's been programmed, I go into the dressing room where Faith Stuart and Amanda Green are already changed into tights and leotards and lacing up their pointe shoes.

We three are the only dancers in the advanced en-pointe class. Faith is still the "new girl" since she only moved here last fall. And although she's in the advanced class, her skill level isn't quite there yet. Still, she's a sweet girl, and it's a relief not to be stuck in this class with only Amanda.

"Oh, there you are," Amanda says when she sees me. "I thought maybe you wouldn't come in today."

"I'm so sorry to hear about your mother." Faith gets up from the bench, coming over to give me a hug.

"Thanks," I murmur after she finally releases me.

"I'm sorry too," Amanda says. "It was so shocking to hear it on the news last weekend. I couldn't believe it was actually your mother, Cleo. You must be totally devastated."

I just nod as I set down my bag and begin to undress.

Amanda and Faith continue to make polite chatter, but when they see I'm not really responding, they excuse themselves to start warming up. I take my time as I gather one leg of my tights into a bunchy "donut." That's a term my mom made up when I was little and trying to figure out how to put on tights without ruining them. I point my toe, slip it into the donut, and feel a lump growing in my throat.

So many things my mom taught me. How will I get along without her?

As I pull on my leotard, adjusting the straps, I feel the need for a pill. I want to block out these memories, to numb this pain. The problem is, I don't have any on me. I had planned to go home and remove one from my secret tampon stash. But thanks to Aunt Kellie, I'm stuck here without any. So for now, I'm on my own.

"Oh, Cleo!" Madame Reginald exclaims when I finally join them in the big open loft. She rushes at me with her wraparound skirt flapping behind her, takes me into her arms, and holds me tight. "I am so very sorry for you loss, chéri!"

"Thank you, Madame," I mutter as I step away. I'm surprisingly comforted to see my ballet instructor. I've known her since I was in preschool, yet she never seems to change or age, and the French accent, which is authentic, never goes away. I think even her perfume is the same—an airy citrus aroma.

"I am so sorry I could not make her funeral." She shakes her head. "I had lessons that morning." She taps her chest. "But my heart was with you."

"Thanks."

"She was a wonderful, wonderful woman." Madame Reginald tucks a loose strand of my hair back into the sloppy bun I made in the dressing room and takes a bobby pin from her own hair to secure it. She sighs sadly. "She will be so very missed!"

"I know."

"So, how are you doing, chéri?" She takes my face in both of her cool hands, looking directly into my eyes. "You are so sad. I know."

"Yeah . . ."

"But *dancing* is like medicine. It is how you will recover from this heartache. Your mother so loved to watch you dance, Cleo. She will be with you in spirit whenever you dance. Don't you think so, too?"

"I hope so."

"Good." She nods firmly, then points to the barre. "Now, warm up, *s'il vous plaît*."

I go through the paces, stretching and warming up, doing pliés, fouettés, jetés, and pirouettes. But my heart is not in it. And then we begin to actually dance, rehearsing our numbers for the June recital, and the steps come automatically to me, but my movements are without life. We are doing *Cinderella* this year, and although I was thrilled to win the lead, there is no passion in my steps as I dance. No one says anything, but I know they are aware of this. Even the janitor who is beginning to sweep on the far side of the room probably knows I have lost the ability to dance.

As we finish the dance where the stepsisters tear up Cinderella's dress, I can see the wheels turning in Amanda's head. And then she begins showing off, doing one perfect fouetté after another, spinning so fast that I feel dizzy, and then just like that she stops.

"How was that?" she asks Madame Reginald.

"Very good." Madame smiles and nods.

"I've been practicing."

"I can see that."

I'm sure Amanda is already planning to replace me as Cinderella — she hates that Madame Reginald picked her to be a stepsister as well as the fairy godmother. For years Amanda and I have competed, and she would love to see me fail at holding on to the lead. That alone should motivate me to try harder. And yet I don't really care.

Madame Reginald says something to the pianist, then instructs Faith and Amanda to begin their stepsister number. She turns to me, asking me to come speak privately with her at her desk.

I follow her, noticing not for the first time how she walks like a real ballerina — straight spine, head high, smooth arms, graceful legs, feet turned out. I try to imitate her.

She sits on the edge of her desk, looking intently at me, as if she'd like to push a magic button that would fix me. Oh, how I wish she could.

"I know you are so sad, chéri."

I bite my lip, feeling the edge of tears, feeling the need for Vicodin.

"How could you not be? But you must use your pain to reach that place in your heart." She taps my sternum with her forefinger. "That secret place where the true dancer lives. You bring her out and you allow her to dance from the depths of your emotion." She strokes my hair. "And you will get well again. I promise."

I wish it were that simple. Not wanting to argue, I simply nod. "I'll try to remember that. My inner dancer."

"And you must practice," she tells me, as if she knows I haven't been.

"Yes."

We do one last number, and I actually try to heed her advice, try to call on my inner dancer; to my surprise, I almost find her. Almost.

"Much better! See, you can do this, chéri." Now she turns to Faith and Amanda. "And you girls were lovely, too. See you all on Tuesday." Then she blows kisses, and we head back to the changing room where the next class, intermediate ballet, is just coming out. They quiet down a little when they see us coming, and as usual, they eye us with respect. I remember doing the same thing when I was younger. Always longing to be one of the advanced ballerinas, wanting to grow up. Now all I want is to turn back the clock.

"Are you going to be okay by the time of the recital?" Amanda asks me as we get dressed.

"What?"

She gives me an innocent look. "Well, you know, you've been through a lot with your mom. And we noticed Madame Reginald talking to you. I'd understand if you needed to step down from—"

"Amanda!" Faith interrupts. "Why are you—?"

"I'm just saying." Amanda holds up her hands. "I'd be willing to step in for you, Cleo. If you needed it."

"*Willing?*" Faith laughs. "You'd plow down Cleo on your way to center stage just to take a bow."

"I would not." Amanda feigns a hurt expression. "That's so not true."

"You've been mad about not getting to play Cinderella for months."

Amanda gives Faith a haughty look now. "I'm not mad. I was disappointed that Madame Reginald favored Cleo. But I'm pretty sure it's only because Cleo is a blonde, and thanks to Disney, everyone thinks Cinderella should be a blonde, which is ridiculous."

"You think I was chosen for my hair color?" Finally I say something.

"I'm just saying." Amanda shrugs as she pulls on a hoodie.

"Cleo got picked because she's the best dancer."

I give Faith a weak smile. "Thanks."

"Or because she's Madame's favorite."

I hurry to button my jeans, wanting out of here, away from Amanda's poison. "You know, I really don't need this right now."

Amanda gives me a somewhat apologetic look. "Yeah, I know. I'm sorry, Cleo. I hadn't really meant to make it sound like that. I was only saying if it's too much for you, I'm willing to learn your dances and step in for you. You know, if you need me to. That's all." She smiles. "No hard feelings, right?"

"Right." I shove my feet into my shoes as I cram my ballet things into my bag. "See you guys later." I pull my hair out of the bun, giving it a shake.

"Sorry about Amanda," Faith says as I head for the door.

"It's okay; I understand." And I do understand. Amanda wants to dance the lead. She's made it clear. And maybe she'll get to. I just don't want to hand it to her on a silver platter. I'd rather let her sweat a little.

I'm just coming out of the stairwell when I spot Daniel standing over by the door. "Hey," I call to him. "Did I keep you waiting?"

"No, it's okay." He comes over to me. "In fact, I hope you don't mind that I snuck upstairs and peeked at you girls while you were dancing."

"Seriously?"

He looks embarrassed. "Is that okay?"

I shrug. "There's no rule against it. A lot of the moms stick around and watch. Not in our class so much, although my mom used to like to watch. She would pretend to knit or read a magazine sometimes, but she was always watching."

"Did that make today hard?" He opens the door for me. "Being there without her?"

I just nod as we go out onto the sidewalk. Swallowing hard and willing myself not to cry, I desperately long for a pill right now.

aniel points to The Coffee Station, a small coffeehouse just down the street. "Is that okay for coffee?"

"Sure." And just like that, we're walking down the sidewalk together. Is this really happening, or am I daydreaming or delusional? I cannot believe I'm with Daniel right now. It is seriously surreal, and I'm tempted to do something really lame like pinch myself.

As he opens the door, a bell jingles and the smell of fresh-roasted coffee and the loud roar of the espresso machine confirm that this is indeed real.

I listen as Daniel places his order and, partly out of nerves and partly because it sounds good, tell the girl I'll have the same. Before long we're seated at a marble-topped table where we make nervous small talk until the girl calls out Daniel's name, and he returns with two black mugs of steaming mocha.

"You're a very good dancer." Daniel smiles as he sets a frothy-topped mug in front of me.

I blink. "You really think so?"

"Absolutely." He nods eagerly. "I mean, I'm no expert and I'm guessing your heart wasn't totally into it, but I could tell you're good."

"Thanks." I explain to him what Madame Reginald told me about finding my inner ballerina.

"That makes sense. Sports can be like that, too. You go to the hard place, and you come back stronger."

"Maybe . . ."

"I really admire you, Cleo."

"Why?"

"You've been through so much, but you do it with . . . with . . ."—he pauses as if searching for the right word—"maybe it's grace. Yeah, you do it with grace. That's really admirable. And cool." He smiles.

I look down at my mocha. If he had any idea . . . if he knew what role I played in my own mother's death, what a horrible daughter, what a spoiled brat I really am . . . well, he probably wouldn't even want to talk to me. And who could blame him?

"So I was determined not to bring you down," he tells me. "And it looks like I've already done that."

I look up at him, longing not to blow this moment, wishing I were someone else or that this were a few weeks earlier. "No, you're not bringing me down. I'm just already there. I'm sorry. I guess I'm not very good company."

"No, you're fine, Cleo." He begins talking about other things, telling me about his plan to work at his dad's radio station this summer.

"Will you be a DJ?"

He chuckles. "I wish. No, I'll be more like a gopher. I work there every summer, and I've only been on the air a few times. But that would be cool."

"You'd probably be good at it. You have a nice voice."

"Thanks." He actually does some little DJ narrative, which is really pretty good.

"Sounds like you've been practicing."

"I keep trying to talk Dad into giving me a chance. You never know."

We continue to talk about nothing and everything, and finally he tells me it's after six o'clock. "Do you need to get home?"

I shrug. "I don't know. Do you?"

"Kind of."

I reach for my bag. "Yeah, my aunt will probably start wondering." Then I tell him about how protective my mom was of me. "And since my aunt is her sister, I suspect she'll pick up where my mom left off."

"That must be nice."

"Nice?" I stare at him in wonder as we both stand. "Are you kidding?"

"My parents got divorced a few years ago."

"Really? I didn't know that."

"It's not big news. Anyway, my mom remarried a guy I don't get along with, so I asked to live with my dad and my mom didn't protest." He opens the door for me.

"Oh . . ." I try to wrap my head around this as we go out. "Do you miss her?"

"Sometimes." He presses his lips together with a frown. "And sometimes I just get really angry at her."

"Angry?"

"You know, for leaving my dad, finding someone else."

"Oh . . . yeah."

"Like maybe it would've been easier if she'd died instead."

I feel slightly stunned by this statement.

"I know, it sounds horrible." We're walking back toward the ballet academy now, and I'm guessing he's parked there. "It's not something I'm proud of or go around saying ever. But it's the truth."

"I think I can understand that." But the truth is, I don't really get this. I would much rather have my mom leave my dad and be alive than the way things are. Still, I'm not going to say that.

"Here we are," he says as we come to a small blue pickup. "My wheels."

"Nice," I say as he opens the passenger door for me. I'm surprised he's such a gentleman, but I appreciate it.

"Not that nice," he says with a grin. "But as my dad tells me, don't look a gift horse in the mouth." He laughs. "Whatever that means."

"I asked my dad if I could have my mom's car," I admit as Daniel turns his key in the ignition. "Now I wonder if that's a mistake."

"Why would it be a mistake?"

"It was . . . you know . . . the last place she was . . . before the murder."

"Oh." He nods with a slight frown. "That could be kind of hard, don't you think?"

"Yeah, I'm kind of rethinking it now. I just thought it'd be good to have my own car."

"Well, if you need a ride, I'm around."

I glance at him, wondering why he's being so nice to me. Is it just pity? His Christian duty? To change the subject, I give him directions to my house. Then we both sit there quietly for a while.

"Am I coming on too strong, Cleo?"

"Too strong?"

"I don't want to scare you away."

"What do you mean? Scare me away?"

"I mean, *I like you*, Cleo."

"Oh." I look straight ahead now. I think I get what he's saying, and a part of me is blown away to hear it. But another part of me is worried, unsure of how to handle this. Is he saying he wants to go out with me? Be my boyfriend? I've never had a serious boyfriend before. But now here I am, with the guy of my dreams—and he's telling me he likes me.

"I am coming on too strong, aren't I?"

"No, I'm just trying to take all this in."

"Unless the rumors were true," he says quietly. "But I never believed them."

"What rumors?" Now I feel nervous. What have people been saying about me?

"Well, a while back, some of the girls—you know how they can be, probably just jealous or something—insinuated that you and Lola were more than just friends."

"What?" I turn to look at him. "What are you saying?"

"I never said it," he says defensively. "And I never believed it either. I'm just saying there was some silly gossip before. And you have to admit that you and Lola have always been really close friends."

"And that's all we ever were, too. Lola was my best friend. And I really miss her."

He laughs. "I figured it was just dumb gossip."

"Well, it's pretty aggravating to hear. I can't believe what some people say about others. And some girls can be so mean."

"I know. It gets old, too. Fortunately I think a lot of them have outgrown it."

"Hopefully."

"So . . . what do you think, Cleo?"

"Think?"

"About what I said. I like you. I'd like to get to know you better. I know you're still getting over the loss of your mom, but do you think you'd want to go out with me . . . sometime?"

I feel seriously dizzy now. I'm not sure if it's low blood sugar, like Aunt Kellie would say, a need for a pain pill, or something much sweeter. "Sure," I tell Daniel, making what I hope is a smile. "I'd like that. But you have to understand that I'm . . . well, I'm not at my best these days. You know?"

He's pulled in front of my house, and I'm slightly surprised that he listened so well to my directions. "I do understand, Cleo." He reaches over and takes my hand, giving it a squeeze. "I'm actually a pretty understanding guy."

Okay, now I'm feeling faint, but I can't imagine how embarrassing it would be to faint right here in his pickup. "That's cool." I reach for the door handle. But before I can even get out of the door, he's dashed around and is helping me.

"My dad taught me to be a gentleman," he says apologetically. "I hope you don't mind.

"Not at all."

He walks me all the way to the front door, and I'm not sure what to do. Do I ask him in? Let him kiss me? What?

"Okay then," he says. "I guess I'll see you tomorrow."

"Okay." I nod.

"And maybe you'd like a ride to school?"

"Sure. That'd be great."

"I know you used to ride with Lola all the time."

"That's right . . . I did."

"Yeah, I know more about you than you thought, huh?" He grins a bit sheepishly. "But really, I'm not a stalker."

"I didn't think you were."

"I've just been waiting for the right moment. So I'll be here a little before eight." He goes down the steps from the porch. "Okay?"

"Perfect." I wave now, then turn and go into the house, where I drop my bag with a thud and let out a squeal of delight.

"What's going on?" Aunt Kellie emerges from the kitchen wearing oven mitts and a worried expression. "What's wrong?"

"Sorry. I was actually just happy."

"Oh?" She looks so startled by this statement that I suddenly feel very guilty. Like who do I think I am to feel this happy? But instead of attempting to explain, I tell her I need to use the bathroom. And she tells me that dinner is ready. I go to the bathroom, but while I'm in there, my mind is occupied with one thing.

I want a pill. And yet I am determined not to give in. I am done with that.

I go to the kitchen, where my aunt is removing a big pan of something yellow from the oven.

"I thought we'd eat in the kitchen tonight," she tells me. "I know your mother liked the dining room, but your dad's work-ing late tonight, and it feels too big for just the two of us, don't you think?"

"Yes." I nod. "Absolutely."

Soon we are seated at the island, and Aunt Kellie bows her head and says a blessing, and I pretend to pray along with her. Then she spoons a big glob of some kind of macaroni casserole onto my plate. "Dig in. This is my famous triple-cheese macaroni-and-cheese dish."

"Oh." I timidly dip my fork into the gooey-looking pasta. My aunt definitely does not get the concept of low carbs and low fat. Something it took me a couple of years to train my mother to understand. But tonight I decide I don't care about it so much. In fact, I surprise myself and her by indulging in a second helping.

"I'm glad you like it," she says happily. "I've been worried that you're not eating enough. You don't look well."

I just ignore this comment. It's something I've heard a lot from her in the past few days.

"How was ballet?" she asks in an obvious attempt to create a conversation.

And, really, I don't know why I'm so hard on her. Well, other than the fact that I'm almost eighteen and do not feel the need to have a babysitter like her twenty-four/seven.

"Okay."

"So . . . you're glad you went?"

"I guess so." I finish off my last bite, pushing my plate away.

She smiles triumphantly. But then she begins to inquire about Daniel, and I tell her I want to go downstairs to practice ballet.

"Oh, that's wonderful, Cleo." She stands and starts clearing the dishes. "I've been worried that you weren't practicing enough. In fact, if you go down and get to work on it, I'll clean this up."

That comment makes me wonder if she expected me to clean up after dinner. But I don't ask. As I go downstairs, I remember how Lola was always surprised when she ate at our house. She couldn't believe my mother never expected me to help in the kitchen, or anywhere else, for that matter. Lola often told me I was spoiled. And I suppose she was right, but being spoiled by my mother came with its own price. Not that I want to think about that.

I'm tempted to call Lola right now. I'd so like to tell her all about Daniel and the things he said to me today. But at the same time I'm worried she'll mention my mother and want to talk about that. So I decide that instead of calling, I'll shoot her an e-mail before I go to bed. That's been our main form of communication lately. And, for me, it's simpler . . . safer.

I flip on the overhead fluorescent lights in the basement. Then I just stand there, staring at my starkly lit image in the mirror. But all I can see is a ghostlike girl and a blank, empty face with two dark holes where my eyes should be. It's like my soul is gone. Like all I can see is wickedness, hypocrisy, deceit. This is not me. And I don't want to be this girl. I want to erase her and start over.

I turn away and change into ballet shoes, then attempt to do some stretches, warming up, doing the normal things. But I feel like the life and energy have been sucked out of me. Like there is nothing left. And all I can think of is my mother and how she is gone and never coming back, and how much I miss her, and how it's my fault she's gone. How I have ruined everything — not only for me but for my dad and my aunt and who knows how many others. I feel like I'm the most worthless person on the planet, like I do not deserve to be alive. I feel like I'm being suffocated by all these heavy layers of guilt.

Trying to shut out this pain, I do a series of pliés, focusing on perfection, feet turned out, knees turned out, slow and grace-ful . . . demi . . . grand . . . but as I go into an arabesque, all I can think about is my mother, how she created this room, how she hand laid each board of this wooden floor, and all I want is to run upstairs and get a pill.

I hold the arabesque, balancing on one leg, the other leg at a right angle, shoulders squared, stretching the line of my body from the tips of my fingers to the pointed toe of my extended leg. *I do not want to take any more pills.* I must quit. I *know* I must quit. Taking pills like that is not who I am. It's not who I want to be. It's not what others expect of someone like me.

I switch legs and do another arabesque, this time reminding myself of this new relationship with Daniel. For that reason alone, I know I must quit the pills. He wouldn't understand my need for something like that. I want to be free of that habit. I need to live my life without that kind of a crutch. But my balance is off, and I stumble to keep from falling. Then I just stand there, feeling like a complete loser. Like I can't do anything right. I'm a failure as a daughter, as a ballerina—I will be a failure as a girlfriend. And although I keep telling myself that I will quit the pills, I know I will fail at that as well.

Because something deep within me is whispering dark tales. I try not to listen, but the voice grows more intense . . . louder . . . until this evil inner demon is screaming at me that I'm going to give in, that I'm going to take the easy route. I'm going to use everything and anything I can to block this pain.

As I turn off the lights, all I can think about is my shrinking stash hidden in the tampon box. All I can think about is how good it will feel when this pain is gone.

By Friday morning, only one week since my mother's death, I know that the only way to survive my life will be with help. And the help I need comes in the form of medication. And really, I rationalize as I wash down a pill with lukewarm tap water, that is what people do to treat pain—take pills. Whether it's physical pain or emotional pain, there is always a pill to help with it. And that is simply what I'm doing. Yes, it's a crutch, but if a person can't walk on her own two legs, sometimes a crutch is needed.

Somehow accepting this as a fact feels liberating. As I carefully dress for school, taking time with my hair and a bit of makeup, I feel like I finally have some control over my life. And I feel confident that I can control my use of self-medication. My only problem is that I have one Vicodin pill left. But I also have the phone number of a guy named T. J. And I've already left him a message, mentioning that Drew gave me his number.

As promised, Daniel picks me up for school in his blue pickup. And feeling like an actor in a movie, I smile at him, act like I'm a normal girl, and manage to make some small talk as he drives us to school.

Then as we go into the building together and he walks me

to my locker, I can feel eyes on me and I can hear some comments about Daniel being with me. But as far as I can tell, no one is mean or catty. My only explanation for their surprisingly good manners is that I'm still getting a sympathy pass.

So goes the day. Daniel and I meet up when we can here and there, and by lunchtime, I even feel accepted by Daniel's friends. It's like I really am a different person. I sit at their table and attempt to be congenial, try to fit in, and at the same time marvel that I am welcome here. What would Lola say? Beneath the surface I am aware that the price I've paid for this kind of acceptance is steep — very steep. But with the help of another pill, I am able to soften the sharp edges of that reality.

I've already checked my phone messages and know that T. J. has returned my call. His message is short, and I can tell he's suspicious. I can't afford to risk calling him back until I'm certain no one is around to overhear me.

After school, Daniel asks me if I want to get coffee again. And despite the nagging need to call T. J., I agree. But after we get to The Coffee Station and order our coffees, I excuse myself to the bathroom, where I quickly call T. J. and he tells me that Drew backed up my story.

"So where do you want to meet?" he asks. "Someplace public but private, if you know what I mean."

I think hard, then finally suggest we meet at the small park in my neighborhood at five o'clock. He tells me to bring cash and not to be late. As I close my phone, I can't help but think how weird and shady this rendezvous sounds, but really, what choice do I have?

By the time I rejoin Daniel, he's already picked up our mochas and is waiting at the same table as yesterday.

"Is this our table now?" I ask in a teasing tone.

He smiles. "Maybe so."

And now, determined to focus the conversation away from me, I ask Daniel all kinds of things about himself. Fortunately he doesn't seem to mind this attention, and the more he talks, the more I like him. And I'm surprised to discover that although we plan to attend different colleges next fall, they are only twenty miles apart. And already Daniel is talking about how we can meet up, like we'll still be together then. It all feels so wonderful, but at the same time, it feels like I'm in a bit of a fog. Yet it's a nice, warm sort of fog.

"Any big plans for Easter this weekend?" Daniel asks me.

"Really? It's Easter already?"

"Yeah, it actually came late this year. I mean, May's just over a week away. Can you believe that?"

I shake my head. "I guess I've kind of lost track of the time lately."

"Not me," he says. "I'm already counting the days until graduation."

"Graduation . . ." I try to wrap my head around that.

He reaches across the table, putting his hand over mine. "It's probably going to be hard not having your mother there."

I sigh. "A lot of things are going to be hard. And I appreciate how understanding you are about . . . well, everything. But sometimes it's easier not to talk about it too much. You know?"

"Yeah." He nods. "I get that."

We talk some more, but our coffees are gone now and I'm thinking I need to figure out a way to get some cash so I can pay T. J. Then I come up with an idea. "Hey, do you mind if I run over to the bank down the street?" I glance at my watch. "I just remembered I need to take care of something before the weekend."

"No problem."

I grab my purse and hurry out, thankful that he didn't offer to come with me, thankful there's a branch of our bank nearby, even more thankful that I have my own savings account. And while my savings are supposed to be for college, if I can't survive my own life, I probably won't be much use at college anyway.

My hands are shaking as I fill out the savings withdrawal form. I have no idea how much these pills are going to cost, but I suspect they won't be cheap. And worried that I could run short, I decide to take out five hundred dollars.

But when the teller counts out my cash, I start to feel a little freaked — like what am I doing?

"Planning a big weekend?" she asks cheerfully.

"Yeah," I lie. "My friend and I are going shopping."

"Ooh." She grins. "Sounds fun."

I put the cash in my purse and hurry back to the coffeehouse where Daniel is talking to a couple of friends, Geoff and Leah. "Hey, we just decided to see a movie tonight. It's an indie film at that new theater in the city," he tells me. "Can you come?"

"Sure." I'm surprised at how easily I say this, and it doesn't escape me that this would not be nearly so easy if my mom were still alive. Not that I want to think about that.

Daniel makes a plan with the others about where we'll meet up, and then I tell Daniel I should probably get home to take care of some things first. But as he drives me home, all I can think is that I'm about to meet up with a drug dealer. And what would Daniel think if he knew?

"See you around six?" he asks me on the porch.

"Sounds good."

He smiles, and my heart does a little flip. As he waves and leaves, I still can't believe that this is real, that this is my life. But as I go inside, I realize that my life has a lot of very strange elements in it . . . a lot of striking contrasts. To my relief, Aunt Kellie doesn't seem to be here. And I almost wonder if she's finally come to her senses and decided to move back home. Except I know she promised my dad she'd stick around while he goes on his next trip, so that means at least two more weeks.

It's still about fifteen minutes until five, so I pace around the house, arguing with myself about what I'm about to do.

Finally it's five minutes until five. With a wad of cash in the pocket of my jeans, I head out, walking quickly to the park. T. J. told me he's tall with dark hair, he'd be wearing a denim jacket, and he's easy to spot. But my legs feel jittery as I make my way toward him, still telling myself I don't have to do this. Except that I do have to do this.

"I'm Cleo," I say quickly.

"Hey, Cleo." He flashes a sleazy smile. "You're a very pretty girl."

I just shrug. "Thanks."

"Are you Drew's girlfriend?"

"No. Did he tell you that?"

"Not exactly. But I could tell he likes you. He told me to treat you right."

"Oh . . ."

"And Drew told me you're dealing with your mom's death. That's gotta be tough."

I relax a little. "Yeah, it is. I, uh, I need help to get through it."

"What kind of help?"

Now, almost like I'm talking to a doctor or a shrink, I spill my story about how I've been taking the Vicodin and how they seem to be helping. "Except that sometimes I feel so fuzzy that

I can't focus. And sometimes I have trouble sleeping at night. I just need something that will block out the pain, you know? But I don't want to be sleepy. I need to have some energy during the day. But I need to sleep at night."

He nods like he's taking this all in. "I think you need a combination of things, Cleo. I'd suggest some weed to relax and—"

"No. I don't want weed. I want legal drugs."

"Legal drugs?" He kind of laughs.

"You know what I mean. Prescription drugs. Can you do that?"

"Hey, you're talking to T. J. I can do anything." His mouth twists to one side, like he's thinking hard. "I know what you need." Then he begins throwing around names like Adderall, Cylert, Xanax, Zoloft, and Luminal, and I honestly have no idea what he's talking about.

"Confused?" he asks.

"Yeah. Pretty much." I glance over my shoulder, worried that someone might see or hear us, but other than a couple of kids on the playground swings, the park is empty.

"Do you trust me, Cleo?"

I blink, wondering why I should trust this complete stranger. Except that I'm desperate. "Yeah . . . I guess so."

"Then I'll put together some things for you and get them to you, like, tomorrow afternoon. Okay?"

"But I'm all out of Vicodin *now*. I'm not sure I can make it until tomorrow without going crazy."

"No problemo." He reaches into a pocket and pulls out a small Ziploc bag of pills. "I just happen to have a starter set." And once again he's tossing out words that mean nothing to me.

"Can you make it simpler? I'm not really an expert at this."

He chuckles, then tells me the red ones are to keep me awake and functioning and the blue ones are to help me sleep. "And the white ones are kind of like Vicodin; they dull the pain."

"How much?" I look longingly at the bag.

"For you?" He narrows his eyes slightly. "A hundred bucks."

"A hundred dollars?" I blink. "For just a few pills?"

"Hey, there's enough to keep you going for three days. It's a bargain."

I have no idea whether he's telling me the truth or just taking advantage of me, but I don't have time to waste. I've got to get ready before Daniel picks me up. "Okay," I say reluctantly. "I'll buy them."

Feeling self-conscious, I turn away from him and pull out my cash. I slip out a hundred-dollar bill and shove the other bills back into my pocket. For all I know this guy could rob me. Maybe he's robbing me right now. What if these are just sugar pills?

"Here you go." I discreetly hand him the bill.

"And here you go." He slips the Ziploc into my hand. "A pleasure doing business with you, Cleo." He pockets my money. "And if you need anything else, you just give me a call." He grins. "You've got my number, babe."

"Will it always cost this much? I mean, there's no way I can afford to pay a hundred dollars every three days."

His dark brows arch. "Oh, there's more than one way to pay for what you need. A pretty girl like you . . ."

A chill of fear runs through me, and I step back from him. "Thanks, T. J.," I say somberly. "I've got to go."

Then as I turn and hurry away, he's laughing like he thinks I'm hilarious. And as I jog toward home, I tell myself I will never, ever do this again. I feel dirty and sickened and ashamed. So ashamed.

However, I'm not ashamed enough to flush the pills down the toilet. I wish I were, but I just can't. I am weak. I am needy. And I just need this little bit of help. I will wean myself from these pills soon, but for now, I need them. The question is, which one do I need tonight?

The white ones look tempting. T. J. said they're like Vicodin. On the other hand, I don't always like that fuzzy, tired feeling. So I decide to go with a red one. I want to be awake and alert for my first date with Daniel.

In a way, this feels like my first date ever. Oh, I've gone out before a couple of times, but not with anyone I cared much for. And they were both dates Lola set up. One during our sophomore year when she had a brief crush on a senior and he talked his friend into being my date. But the evening was a disaster—both guys acted like perverts, and that night set both Lola and me back about a year in dating. The next time was last summer when Lola wanted to go out with a guy from her work. We made it a foursome, and although it wasn't as bad as the pervert dudes, it was a disappointment.

But tonight will be different. And maybe I'm getting some help from that little red pill, or maybe I'm just feeling good, but I have high hopes as I crank up my CD player and get dressed. By the time I'm doing a final check in the mirror, I feel like dancing. I'm wearing a top Lola gave me, one my mother thought was too tight. But I'm not going to think about that tonight. Tonight is for having fun.

It's nearly six o'clock when I head out of my room. I still feel like dancing, but I hear someone rustling around in the kitchen, so I control myself. When I peek around the corner, I see my dad putting some bags on the table. He jumps when he sees me.

"Sorry," I say. "I didn't mean to scare you."

"I didn't think you were home." He shoves something behind his back.

I tilt my head, trying to see what he's hiding, but then I spy what looks like a bag of plastic Easter grass and some other Easter goodies in the bag and I think I know. "Uh-oh," I say as I turn around. "Wouldn't want to catch the Easter Bunny on his night off."

Dad chuckles. "You know how your mom . . . used to like to . . ."

I take in a deep breath. "Yeah, I know."

"It's kind of silly, but—"

"No, it's not silly, Dad. It's sweet."

Just then the doorbell rings, and I quickly explain that I'm going to a movie with some friends.

"That's nice." And Dad seems genuinely pleased. "I'm glad to see you getting back to your normal life, Cleo. It's a comfort."

"Yeah, Mom would probably like that."

"You have fun now."

"Thanks." I hold up my bag. "And I have my phone, you know, if you need to reach me."

"And I'll be here," he promises.

I go over and kiss him on the cheek, and he looks surprised since that's not something I usually do. "Love you, Dad," I call as I walk to the door.

"Love you too, Cleo."

His words are still echoing inside my head. *"Glad to see you getting back to your normal life . . . your normal life . . ."*

Like that's even possible anymore.

As I open the front door, I repress all thoughts of elusive normality. But I'm glad to see Daniel standing there. And judging by his expression, he's glad to see me too. "Hey, you're Mr. Punctuality," I tell him.

"I was hoping there'd be enough time for me to meet your dad."

"Uh, yeah, sure." I open the door wider. "Come on in."

Now I'm a little uneasy because I never actually told my dad this was a real date. Not that it should matter much to him. After all, he is my dad . . . not my mother. So I take Daniel into the kitchen where Dad is just popping a yellow Peep into his mouth, and I quickly make an introduction.

"Excuse me," Dad says as he quickly chews, brushes the sugar off his fingers, then shakes hands with Daniel. "Pleased to meet you."

"I know I've seen you in church before," Daniel tells him. "But I don't think we've actually met."

"No." Dad studies Daniel carefully, and I can tell he approves. "I don't think we've have. Thanks for taking the time to meet me tonight."

"And I promise to have your daughter back home by eleven,"

Daniel tells him respectfully. "Is that okay?"

"I appreciate that." Dad nods, then holds out the open box with a sheepish grin. "Care for a Peep?"

I can't help but giggle as Daniel carefully pulls out a bright yellow Peep.

"How about you, Cleo?"

I shake my head. "No thanks, Dad. I think I'll wait for Easter."

Then Daniel and I leave, and soon he is driving us into the city. For a brief moment it hits me—only one week but another lifetime ago, Lola and I were merrily riding the metro into the city. But I block these thoughts out, focusing instead on Daniel as I chatter nonstop about everything and nothing, just filling the air with words.

"You seem pretty happy tonight," he tells me as we're walking to the café where we planned to meet Leah and Geoff.

"It's weird, but I feel happy. I think it might be the weather." Then worried that I might seem callous since it's been only a week since my mom died, I add, "My mother always loved this time of year. It's like I can kinda feel her spirit in the air."

"Cool."

While we have a light dinner with Geoff and Leah, I can tell I'm far more animated than usual. And even though I try to subdue myself and slow it down and just plain shut up, I can't. It's like I've had too much coffee. Like I'm wired. That little red pill!

Suddenly I remember a certain ballet—*The Red Shoes*. The girl puts on those pretty red shoes and cannot stop dancing. Red shoes . . . red pill . . . I cannot stop talking. And yet everyone at the table seems to be interested in my babbling, like I must be entertaining, and it's kind of fun being the center of attention like this.

Even so, I'm relieved when we're finally inside the theater, a cool old building that's been totally restored. And I'm hoping that sitting in a semidark place will help me calm down. But I can't slow down this feeling. The plush seat beneath me feels like a million tiny needles poking through my clothes and into my skin. I want to squirm and twist, and I can feel my hands trembling and my heart racing wildly, kind of like it's going up and down on a roller coaster. What if I have a heart attack? I mean, I have no idea what was actually in that expensive red pill. What if it's something really dangerous?

So instead of enjoying the film, which from time to time looks interesting, I obsess over my health, what I've done, and the fact that I cannot seem to sit still. It's like my skin is crawling, and I'm afraid I might stand up and scream. I feel tortured. And yet a part of me likes it, too. Like it compels all my senses to ride this roller coaster, like it's blocking everything else out.

After what feels like ten years, the movie finally ends and the lights, which seem garishly bright, come on. Then we go outside, where I feel like everything inside of me is shaking uncontrollably. Fortunately no one else seems to notice. We stand out on the sidewalk, where the others critique the movie. And I pretend to agree or disagree. But the truth is, I cannot remember a thing about it. Then Geoff and Leah suggest we go and get some coffee and dessert.

Daniel peers curiously at me. "You look like you've already had too much caffeine," he teases.

"Maybe so." Then I lie and say that I had a couple more cups of coffee at home. "I feel like I'm supercharged."

They laugh like this is funny, although I know it's not. But Daniel's expression is hard to read, like maybe he's wondering if something is really wrong with me. So I decide to play the sympathy card once again. "I guess I was worried about being in the city tonight," I say quietly, eyes downward. And really, this is not completely untrue . . . just insincere.

"Oh, that's right," Daniel says quickly. "What happened . . . I mean to your mom . . . it wasn't too far from here . . ."

Leah puts a hand on my shoulder. "I forgot about that too, Cleo. It was in the city, wasn't it?"

I nod without speaking.

"And it's only been a week," Daniel adds.

"Poor Cleo." Leah wraps her arm around me on one side.

"We'll take care of you." Daniel puts an arm around me on the other side, and Geoff stands close by with an understanding expression. And it's amazing—I feel protected and circled by love.

"You need friends at a time like this," Geoff tells me.

"And you've got us," Leah says.

"Thanks." I'm actually blinking back tears now.

For a while we stand out there in our tight little circle, just talking about life and death and how we all need friends. And it's weird. For the first time, I actually feel like I might survive this. The buzzed feeling is starting to let up a little, and I feel pretty good. But when we get coffee, I opt for decaf. We sit and visit some more. Then Daniel announces it's time to go, and as promised, he gets me home by eleven.

Once again, he walks me to the front door. But this time he lingers on the porch. He slips his arm around me and pushes a strand of hair out of my eyes. "You're really special, Cleo. I can't believe it took until the end of our senior year to figure this out. But I'm glad we did." He leans forward and I'm sure he's going to kiss me, and I'm so excited (and still a little buzzed) that I can't even think what to do. But he stops midway and looks into my still-open eyes, which I should've shut. Instead he simply takes my chin in his hand, gently kissing my forehead, which actually tickles and makes me giggle.

"We'll save more for later," he says in a slightly formal way. Then he bows and tells me good night. As I open the door and go into the house, it feels like I'm walking on air. I go into the family room, where a baseball game is blasting on the big screen and my dad is snoring in his recliner. I lean over and kiss him on the cheek—that's twice in one day—and he sleepily opens his eyes.

"You made it home," he says groggily, almost as if he was worried that, like my mom, I might not.

"Yeah, it was a nice evening. Good night, Daddy."

He gives a weary-looking half smile. "Night, Cleo."

I'm exhausted but still feel shaky as I get ready for bed. I'm way too jittery to sleep. And I wonder just how long this little red pill is going to keep doing its stuff. Finally I can't stand being trapped in this small space, so I tiptoe back out and, seeing Dad's abandoned recliner, quietly go down to the basement, turn on the lights, and dance. I dance and I dance and I dance—just like the girl in the red shoes.

Until finally I'm so exhausted that I collapse on the rose velvet couch. My mother's couch. She found it at a garage sale a few years ago, and I told her it looked like a granny couch. But she insisted it would be perfect in my dance studio. As I snug my head into one of the floral pillows, I smell my mother's scent. I remember how she used to sit down here, pretending to read a book as she watched me practicing. And suddenly, almost as if I've just seen her ghost, I feel wide awake again. But I'm too tired to dance. And too wired to sleep. Wired and tired . . . and miserable.

I tiptoe back up the stairs and go to my room, where I find my baggie of costly pills, still safely nestled where I hid them in the trusted tampon box. I unzip the baggie and remove a blue pill. Blue is for sleep, T. J. told me. Then using the last dregs of some flat soda that's been sitting by my bed for a couple of days, I swallow it down.

Holding my breath I wait expectantly, but nothing happens. I get up and start pacing again, impatiently waiting for this pill to kick in and perform its magic. Then just as I'm about to give up on the stupid blue pill, something hits me. It's like I've been hit by a padded sledgehammer, and I tumble to my bed just in time to blissfully fade out.

· · · · · · · · · ·

The weekend comes and goes in a blur of red, white, and blue—and I'm not talking about the American flag. My primary focus is to balance out these pills, figuring out when to take them, when not to take them, how much is enough, how much is too much. Daniel texts me on Saturday morning, saying his dad insisted on taking him and his sister to visit their grandmother for the weekend. And Aunt Kellie went home to spend time with Uncle Don. So it's been pretty quiet around here with just Dad and me. He sleeps a lot, and I'm consumed with my pills and dancing. I've decided that I like the energy the red pills give me—and dancing is a great way to take the edge off.

By Sunday afternoon, Dad and I are both sugared out and sick of Easter candy, so we agree to have canned soup for dinner. As we're eating, I offer to drive him to the airport. I know he has a red-eye flight that leaves close to midnight, but I suddenly feel possessive of him—I don't want him to leave.

"Aunt Kellie plans on playing chauffeur tonight," he tells me as he rinses the bowls and I put them in the dishwasher. It's weird helping like this in the kitchen, but without Mom or Aunt Kellie around, it's not like the housework is going to do itself.

"I don't mind driving you," I say as I close the dishwasher door.

"It's too late for you to be out. Remember, you have school in the morning."

"But I could drop you off at the airport earlier. Maybe I could go in with you and we could get coffee or —"

"No, Cleo. I don't want you driving through the city by yourself. Not at night."

Now there's a heavy silence, and I know we're both thinking about Mom. Dad is missing her . . . I am feeling guilty.

"So are you all ready to go?" I ask him.

"I guess so." He gives the countertop a swipe with a sponge, then tosses it into the sink with a frown.

"How did you do . . . packing for yourself?" I ask with caution. I know how my mother used to take great care in getting everything ready for him to go on a trip. She'd take care of every last detail, including filling small travel bottles with his favorite shampoo and conditioner and putting them in a zipped baggie for his carry-on case.

He sadly shakes his head. "Your mom spoiled me, Cleo."

"I know." I sigh. "She spoiled me, too."

"I'm just not sure how we'll get along without her —" His voice cracks, and he looks close to tears now.

I can't stand to see him cry. "We'll be okay. I'll learn to help out more."

He just nods, then picks up the newspaper and goes into the family room. But as he sits down in his recliner, holding the paper in front of him, I hear the sound of some choked sobs — sobs that slice through me like a knife.

This is all my fault. My selfishness dismantled our family . . . destroyed our home. As I hurry to my room, all I can think of is taking a pain pill. Something to take away this anguish.

Already my supply has dwindled. And yet the thought of calling T. J. and spending more of my savings on *this crud* makes me want to beat my head against the wall. Or maybe that's what I'm already doing.

I hold up the wrinkled baggie, staring at the remaining pills, wondering how it's possible that something so small costs so much. And yet I understand. For me, these little pills are the difference between sinking and swimming. Without them there's a stone strapped to my chest, and I am sinking to the bottom of the ocean. With them I can float, I can keep my nose above water.

I take a pain pill, then lie down on my bed, waiting for that soft, fuzzy feeling to return . . . taking me away. Away to a place where girls don't murder their mothers . . . a place where nothing matters. Not even the unfinished homework still in my bag. Nothing but nothingness is here.

I wake with a start, sitting up with a strong sensation that something is wrong. Terribly wrong. The lights are out, and I try to grasp where I am and what's happening and why I feel so freaked. The clock by my bed shows it's just a little past midnight. And I remember that my dad's supposed to fly out tonight. Why didn't he come in and tell me good-bye? Or maybe he did. Maybe I was sleeping too soundly to respond.

I tiptoe out to see that Aunt Kellie's car is parked in front of the house, so she must be back from taking him to the airport. I see a crack of light under the door to the guest room; she's probably reading in bed. But still I feel uneasy, like something bad has happened or is about to happen. And yet everything in our house seems normal. Or as normal as it can be, considering the past week.

I open the door to my parents' room — rather my dad's room — and this space looks a lot messier than usual. The unmade bed, clothes strewn about, shoes here and there, closet doors gaping open. Nothing seems particularly amiss, just the effects of my dad's lack of housekeeping skills.

I go into the bathroom to see more of the same. Shaving stuff on the counter, whiskers in the sink, toothpaste tube open, blue goo dripping onto the countertop. I can't even imagine what my mother would think to see her pretty bathroom like this. Perhaps she wouldn't care anymore. Why should she?

I put the lid on Dad's cologne. A woodsy fragrance my mother picked out for him. But the smell of it sends another wave of fear through me. What if I never see him again? What if his plane goes down? What if he's murdered? What if I'm left all alone in the world? No mother, no father . . . just Aunt Kellie, which is little consolation.

My heart is pounding with this anxiety. And although it makes no sense, I have a strong feeling that this is my fate. Both my parents taken from me — a punishment for my stupidity, my selfishness, my lies.

I turn away and rush from their room, hurrying back to my own room, where I swallow a blue pill and wait for it to deliver me from the harsh reality of my life.

If only it could last forever.

On Monday afternoon, I meet T. J. in the park again. This time the price is higher, but the reward is more pills. And as I walk back to my house, I tell myself that I will make this supply last longer. Not only that, but I will kick this dirty little habit. *I will.* Just one more week and I will free myself from this pathetic crutch forever. I just can't function without my pills right now. And okay, there's another whisper inside of me, saying that I cannot function *with* them either. But I am not listening.

These pills are not red, white, and blue like the old ones. But T. J. separated them into different baggies, explaining which ones did what, and I think I understand. Like my mother used to say, "You are your own best doctor." However, I'm pretty sure this is not what she had in mind.

For the next week, I fall into a slightly comfortable pattern. I take a pill to wake me up in the morning and another one to help me dance in the afternoon. Then there's a pill to help me forget — to block out the pain as needed — and a different one, sometimes two, to knock me out at night. And then the same thing all over again the next day. So I go day after day after day, and sometimes one pill becomes two pills, but I'm holding it right there. I haven't taken three pills at once, and I don't plan to do that.

And really, it's not such a bad way to live. Except that sometimes it seems the only thing I'm thinking about is when I'll take the next pill. I count the minutes on the clock, trying to make myself wait. But sometimes it's just too hard, and I give in. And then I obsess over how many pills I have left and wonder how I can afford to buy another batch next week. Then I tell myself I won't need them next week. But I'm just lying to myself. I do the math in my head, figuring how many pills cost how many dollars, and I try to estimate how long my savings will last if this continues.

· · · · · · · · ·

On Thursday, nearly two weeks after my mother was murdered, I am telling myself that I have to kick this habit. I go a whole day without taking a single pill. But by the time I'm at ballet, I feel myself slowly slipping away. It's like I'm falling apart. And everyone around me can see it, too.

"What is wrong with you?" Amanda demands after I nearly plow her over doing a series of out-of-balance fouettés.

"Sorry. I'm a little clumsy today."

"A *little*?" She indignantly smoothes her sleek dark hair back into place, then adjusts a strap on her leotard. "Are you sure you can dance the lead, Cleo? Because as I've told you, I'm perfectly willing to step in." Amanda announces this loudly enough for Madame Reginald to hear.

"What's this?" Madame comes over to us. "What are you saying, Amanda?"

"I was simply telling Cleo that I am willing to dance the

lead if she's not up to it."

"Of course she's up to it," Madame assures her.

"You obviously didn't see her trample me just now." Amanda gives Madame a wounded look. "She rolled over me like a bull-dozer. I'm just lucky she didn't give me a black eye."

Madame smiles patiently. "Perhaps we all simply need to give each other a bit more space."

"That might keep me safe for now." Amanda steps away from me like I'm contagious. "But what about during the recital? That's not a huge stage, you know. What if Cleo knocks down other dancers? What if she ruins the whole evening for everyone?"

"Fine," I snap at Amanda. "Go ahead and dance the lead." Then I storm out.

My hissy fit is a response to her nasty comments, but I know what's really going on. I just want out of here so I can take a pill. I need something to energize me and pep me up. Feeling like a slug with six feet, I struggle back into my street clothes, then make a getaway before Madame or Faith has a chance to stop me.

Out on the street, I realize it's too early for Daniel to pick me up yet. He has a graduation planning meeting until five. But I'm actually relieved not to face him. I'd hate for Daniel to see me like this. He's already made a couple of comments about how my moods seem to go up and down a lot. He's been under-standing and says it's just part of my grieving process, but I'm worried he might become suspicious. And as much as I like him, I'm not sure I can juggle a boyfriend with my need for these pills. It's possible I'll have to let one of them go.

I consider walking home, but that will take half an hour. And my feet already feel like they're wearing cement shoes. So I call my aunt, begging her to come get me. "I just can't dance today."

"What's wrong?"

"I just need to come home!"

"Are you okay, Cleo?"

"It's just a bad headache," I say, which is not entirely false. "I need to lie down." I make a pathetic groan, and Aunt Kellie promises to be here within minutes. I hang up and then call and leave a message for Daniel. And as I wait for my aunt's ugly van, my head really does start to throb.

As she drives us home, Aunt Kellie seems extra quiet and somewhat distracted. This is so not her. And suddenly I'm worried. What if she found my stash of pills? What if she knows? What if she called my dad and told him that his daughter is hooked on drugs?

"I have something I need to talk to you about," she says quietly as she parks her van in the driveway.

"What?" I nervously ask.

"We can talk in the house."

Now I *know* she found my pills. Why else would she be acting so weird? She was probably "cleaning" my room today, which I've clearly told her not to do anymore. But she probably did it anyway. And then she probably got to snooping while she was in there. She seems like the snoopy type. And now she knows what I've been doing. As I go into the house, I feel certain of it. She knows.

"Come into the kitchen," she tells me as I'm about to sneak off to my room — eager to see if the pills are gone.

"Just a minute," I say in a grumpy tone.

"No, Cleo. Please, come in here now. I *really* need to talk to you."

I give her a smoldering look, then reluctantly follow her.

"I know how you can be." She turns on the teakettle. "You will go into your room and never come out again."

"But I have this headache. I want to—"

"Here." She reaches into the cabinet where my mother always kept a few first-aid things and over-the-counter medicines. "Take some ibuprofen." She sets the bottle on the counter, fills a glass of water, then sets it in front of me. "And drink all that water. It will help."

I shrug as I pry open the bottle, shake out two capsules, pop them into my mouth, and wash them down with water. Then I stare at her with my darkest look, waiting for her to blast me with her discovery. Just get it over with.

"I don't really know where to begin." A deep *V* creases her brow. "But I need to just get this out in the open, Cleo."

I hold my breath now, bracing myself for her accusation, trying to prep my brain to work out some line of defense. Maybe I can tell her that Lola left that box of tampons in my room. I'll act dumb and say they aren't even mine. Yes, that's what I'll do. It's amazing how easy it is to lie . . . once you get started. The tricky part is trying to remember which lies you've actually told.

"There was a . . . well, a rather odd message on the answering machine today."

I frown, trying to grasp what she is saying. Did T. J. call here? Did he ask about meeting me in the park? Did he mention doing a drug deal? And why would he do something so totally stupid?

"I guess I should just come out with it." She has a confused expression. "But I confess it's got me completely bewildered."

My fists are clenched as I wait for her to get this over with, trying to corral my explanation and make it more believable.

Like Lola brought those tampons here when she spent the night, then forgot them the next day when she left for California. And how I just stuck them in a drawer and forgot about them. I imagine how I can make a really shocked expression. But Aunt Kellie is talking again, and I missed the first part of what she said.

"So it was from your mother's friend."

"Huh?" Now I'm totally lost.

"Trina. The one who got married recently."

"Who got married?"

"Remember? *Trina.* She had that bachelorette party. On the night your mother was . . . uh, killed."

"Trina?"

Aunt Kellie nods. "She left a message."

"She called here at the house?"

"Yes. She left a message for your dad. But, of course, I heard it when I played back the messages after I got back from getting groceries this morning."

"Right . . ." I nod, still trying to grasp this. "Trina called and left a message. But I don't get it. Why are you so upset?"

"You need to hear this message." Aunt Kellie goes over to our answering machine. She pushes a button, skips a couple of old messages, and then I hear a female voice.

*"Hello, Hugh. This is Trina Billings. I recently got back from my honeymoon, and I, uh, I heard the terrible news about Karen. I'm just so sorry. I can't even say how sorry I am. Sorry and sad. But I'm also quite confused, Hugh. You see, my sister saved everything that was in the newspaper in regard to Karen's murder. And I read it last night, but it just doesn't add up."* She clears her throat. *"Now, I realize you were on a business trip, but you probably were aware that Karen came to my bachelorette party that night — the*

*night it happened. And she didn't stay late either. She wanted to go home to be with Cleo since you were away from home. But the newspapers say Karen was murdered in the city. And the city, as you know, is two hours away from Riverside. I just don't understand why she would've gone there late at night."*

There's a long pause, and I wonder if that's it. But I can tell by Aunt Kellie's face, there is more.

*"And certainly, I don't want to trouble you about this, Hugh, but it's just been nagging me all night long and I can't figure it out. It's so odd. And I understand that you probably have a lot on your mind, but if you have time, I'd like to hear what really happened and why she was in the city that night. Again, I am so sorry for your loss. Karen was one of the sweetest and finest people I know. I just don't understand. So please give me a call."* And then Trina rattles off a phone number.

"See?" Aunt Kellie turns to me with a perplexed expression. "I just can't make heads or tails of it. Can you?"

I do not know what to say. I almost wish the message had been from T. J. now. I wish he'd called and talked about selling me drugs. Really, that would be preferable to this.

"Why would your mother drive all the way from Riverside to go into the city that night?" Aunt Kellie looks truly bewildered. "It really doesn't make sense. I can understand why Trina called. It's just so very odd."

Okay, I'm trying to think fast now. Something . . . anything . . . to shift this blame away from me. "Well," I begin slowly, "it was Trina's wedding the next day. Maybe Mom went to the city to get her a present."

"But the wedding present is still here. It's in a cupboard in the laundry room, all wrapped, with a card and everything. In fact, I've been meaning to figure out how to get it to Trina and her husband."

"Oh . . ." I nod, still trying to think of something. "Maybe Mom wanted to buy a new dress."

"A new dress?" Aunt Kellie looks skeptical.

"Well, that night—you know, before she went to the party—she was kind of going through her closet, searching for something to wear, and she wasn't too happy with the choices. Maybe she decided she needed something more fashionable to wear to the wedding."

"I don't know . . ." Aunt Kellie is unconvinced.

"That *might* be it," I continue. "Especially after she saw her old college friends at the party. She might've realized that she really did need something prettier for the wedding."

"Even so, wouldn't she have asked you to go with her? Trina said she left early to come home and be with you. Besides that, what kind of stores would be open that late at night? And you know how your mother hated going into the city in the daytime, let alone at night. Trina is right. It just doesn't add up."

Now I frown at my aunt. "So what do you think? Why would my mom go to the city like that?"

She slowly shakes her head. "If it was anyone else . . . I mean, anyone besides Karen who'd gone into the city late at night and got caught in foul play, well, I might be suspicious."

"*Suspicious?*"

"You know. If it was *someone else*. Not your dear, sweet mother. I might suspect another person's character. I might suspect that person might be having some kind of clandestine meeting. An illicit affair or blackmail or a drug deal." She grimaces. "But that's the result of reading too many mysteries. Because I know beyond a shadow of a doubt that your mother would never ever have been involved in anything shady like that."

"No, of course not."

"Anyway, I just thought you should know about the message."

"Yeah . . ." I rub my head now, which is actually hurting quite a bit.

"Oh, dear, I forgot all about your headache." She frowns. "You really don't look well, Cleo. Maybe you should go lie down."

"I think I'll do that." I turn to go.

"One more thing."

I wait, once again bracing myself for additional bad news. Like maybe she really did discover my drug stash after all. But maybe I don't care anymore. Maybe the whole world is about to come crashing down on my aching head anyway.

"I'm just not sure what to tell your dad."

I turn to peer at her. "Tell him *what*?"

"What Trina said." She cocks her head to one side, looking at me like she's questioning my intelligence. "Her message on the answering machine."

"Oh . . . yeah."

"It's just that I hate to worry him with this. I mean, while he's on his business trip. He probably needs to stay focused, don't you think? Do you suppose it can wait until he gets home?"

I shrug. "I don't see why not."

"Yes. That's what I thought."

I feel a tiny morsel of relief as I go to my room. At least she's not calling Dad with this news right now. That buys me a bit of time to figure things out. Also, she seems completely oblivious to my dirty little secret. Still, I have a strong sense that it's all just a matter of time before this fragile house of lies comes crashing down on me.

If only it could bury me alive.

## CHAPTER 16

**D**espite my resolve to quit these pills, I need them more than ever now. And I don't think twice about meeting T. J. at the park on Saturday morning for a new supply. Although I resent the way he acts like he's my new best friend, I try not to let on. I try to act pleasant, hoping he'll take pity on me and reduce his price. But when he suggests "other ways" that I can get a discount, I feel like punching him. And when he tries to lure me to his derelict car to "party" with his loser buddies, I feel like I could hurl all over his ugly leather jacket.

"You can turn your nose up at me now," he yells as I hurry away. I'm clutching my baggie like it's full of diamonds. "But just you wait—you'll come begging, Cleo. You'll get down on your knees for me." He lets out a wicked laugh that sends a cold shock wave running through me.

I start to jog now, telling myself over and over, *This is the last time . . . the last time.*

I can't keep living like this. Not that this is living. It isn't. I would rather be dead. Except that now I'm not sure where I'd go when I die. I used to believe I'd end up in heaven, where I'm sure my mother must be right now. But now I feel certain that I am destined for hell. And that scares me.

Apparently it doesn't scare me enough. Because another week passes, a week that is frighteningly similar to the previous week. But even more freaky is that I barely even notice. It's like I've tumbled into this rut — or perhaps it's the gutter or a deep, deep ditch — and I can't climb out. And I can't believe that no one seems to notice my fall. Or maybe they do, but I'm just so spaced out I can't tell. So turn the days of my life.

Dad's still on a trip. Aunt Kellie is baking casseroles. Daniel's talking about college. And I am buying illegal drugs from a thug in the park down the street. For all I know, T. J. could be connected to the "druggie" who murdered my mother. Or wait . . . maybe that's me.

My life has been shattered into dozens of jagged little pieces of guilt, shame, deceit, regret, pain, sadness, lies, loss, hypocrisy, selfishness, addiction, denial, fear, and despair. All the good parts seem to be missing, and I doubt I can find them. Even if I could, I don't think I can ever put myself back together again. And sometimes, like late at night when I can't sleep, it is very tempting to just swallow all those pills and escape permanently. Except for that big question that hangs over my head like the blade of a guillotine: *Where will I end up?*

So I take pills that buzz me into an energetic frenzy, which allows me to dance and dance until my heart is racing and my hands are shaking and I feel like I will throw up or pass out . . . or just die.

I was relieved when Daniel told me he'd be gone this weekend. His dad is taking him to visit the college campus where he'll be going next fall. Daniel invited me to come along, but I couldn't walk that tightrope — balancing my need for my pills with being a "normal" girlfriend around him and his dad. I told Daniel it's because my own dad is coming home this weekend.

But the truth is, I am not looking forward to seeing my dad now. Although I've concocted a reasonable excuse for why my mom was in the city the night she was killed, I don't know if I can make him believe me.

"Do you want to go with me to the airport to get your dad?" Aunt Kellie asks on Saturday afternoon.

"I don't think so," I say as I get a glass of water. I'm wearing my tights and leotard. "I need to practice."

She nods like this is a good excuse. "I've got dinner in the oven, but if you'd like to set the table . . ."

Out of habit, I frown like this is a great imposition. But then I remember my resolve to help out more. "Sure, I can do that."

She looks relieved. And as soon as she's gone, I set the table, whirling about the dining room like a dancing busboy, getting everything just so. I even put out the cloth napkins—although Aunt Kellie prefers paper—and fold them exactly like my mother used to do. Then I head back to the basement and dance and dance until I'm too tired to think and it feels like I'm about to have a heart attack.

The next thing I know, my aunt calls down saying it's time for dinner and my dad is home. I drag myself back up the stairs. It's weird because while part of me feels like I'm still buzzing, another part is so heavy I can barely move my feet.

"Are you okay?" my aunt asks me with a furrowed brow.

I just nod. "I'll change clothes," I mumble as I head for my room. But once the door is closed to my room, I go for my stash of pills. But this time I don't know which one to take. It's like I'm so numb, I can't even figure out what I need. More energy? Less pain? To sleep? I'm tempted to take a handful, but my dad just got home. I haven't seen him for two weeks. I can do better than this.

I take two pain pills and struggle to peel off my sweaty

dance clothes. Then I struggle even more to get dressed, just sitting there with one leg in my jeans and the other one still bare.

Finally Aunt Kellie knocks on my door, saying it's time for dinner.

I blink at my strange-looking image in the mirror, pull on my jeans, and tell her I'm coming. Then, feeling hazy, like this is a dream, I make my way to the dining room and sit in my regular place. At least I think it's my regular place. My head is kind of spinning now.

"Are you all right?" my dad asks with worried eyes.

"I don't . . . know."

My aunt comes over and puts her hand on my forehead. "You don't look well, Cleo."

"I . . . I'm tired," I mumble. "Too much . . . dancing."

"She's been dancing a lot lately, practicing for the recital," my aunt tells my dad. "Probably overdoing it."

"You look like you've lost weight."

I just nod at Dad, but the motion makes me feel woozy, and I think I'm about to fall out of my chair or vomit. "I . . . I . . . don't feel too good."

"Come on." Aunt Kellie helps me to my feet. "Let's get you back to your room. I'll bring your dinner in there."

"I'm not hungry."

"You have to eat something," she insists.

Soon I'm sitting up in bed and there's some food on a tray in front of me. I poke something brownish with my finger, then lean my head back and sigh.

"Something is wrong with you." My aunt bends over and peers into my eyes.

"I'm just tired."

Her eyes are narrowed, studying me like I'm a bug under a magnifying glass. "If I didn't know better, I'd say you were using drugs, Cleo. Your pupils are dilated and—"

"That's ridiculous." I attempt a laugh, but it sounds more like a cough.

"You're not taking drugs, *are you?*"

"Of course not." Now I close my eyes. "I'm just tired. And sad. My mom died, *remember?*"

"Yes. My sister died, too." I hear her leave, but when I look up, I see she left my door open. I want to get up and close it, shut her out, but my legs feel like they're encased in thick mud. And I am so tired . . . dizzy . . . fuzzy . . . blurry.

Later that evening, after it's dark outside, my dad comes into my room. He removes the tray of barely touched food and just looks at me. His eyes are red and puffy, like he's been crying. "I shouldn't have gone on that business trip. It was too soon to leave you alone like that, Cleo. I'm so sorry. Can you forgive me?"

I blink and stare at him. Does he really think this is his fault? Seriously, his fault? If only he knew.

"My work has taken me away from my family for too long," he continues. "And now it's taking my family away from me. Too much to pay for too little return . . . bad investment . . . risky business."

"Huh?" I'm trying to understand what he's saying, but it doesn't quite make sense.

"My work took me away from your mom—" His voice breaks. "If I'd been home, she'd probably still be alive."

I nod, taking this in. "Yeah . . . maybe so." But I know it's not true. And I cannot admit the part I played.

"And then I left you alone, and Kellie says you need me to be here."

The guilt is burying me, suffocating me. I want to tell Dad I'm sorry, that it's all my fault, confess everything, but it's like I'm frozen, stuck. I can't speak, can't think, can barely even breathe.

Dad takes my hand in his. "I need you to get through this, Cleo. And I want to help you. I'm going to cancel my next consulting trip and just—"

"No," I say quickly. "You don't need to cancel your trip. Not for me."

"But look at you." He wipes his wet cheeks with his hands. "You are falling apart. Aunt Kellie is really worried about your health, sweetheart. So am I."

"I just need some rest. I'm tired; that's all."

He nods. "Okay. You get some sleep. We can talk about this tomorrow. Aunt Kellie wants us to go to church with her in the morning, and I think it's about time we went back. Your mother would want us to go to church. I was foolish to stop. Foolish and selfish. I'm sorry, Cleo. I'll do better."

I don't respond . . . just close my eyes . . . wishing this to be over.

"And then, after church tomorrow, we'll go to the cemetery."

"The cemetery?" I open my eyes. *"Why?"*

He sniffs, then wipes his nose with a tissue. "It's Mother's Day tomorrow. We'll take your mom some roses. Pink roses. Her favorite."

"Oh . . ." It feels like a bag of stones is on my chest, pushing the air from my lungs.

"You rest, honey. We'll do better. Tomorrow's a new day."

"Yeah . . . tomorrow . . . Mother's Day . . ."

My dad leaves the room, shutting the door.

I sit up and struggle to breathe. My heart is racing again, yet all I've been doing is lying here. I take not one but two sleeping pills, hoping to slow things down. But as I lie here, I wonder if these drugs are killing me. And why should I even care?

## CHAPTER 17

This morning I get up and tell myself that I'll quit these pills today — once and for all, I want to end this madness. But the thought of attending church as well as visiting my mother's grave — on *Mother's Day* — undoes me. My good intentions are tossed aside, and I succumb to the lure of the contents of a Ziploc baggie. As I take both a pain pill and an amphetamine, I feel weak and pathetic and hopeless.

As a result, I feel numb and dazed and barely present during the church service. The music and the words go right over my head, floating around with the dust particles that sparkle in the sunlight. It all just whooshes away. All except for one part of the sermon that somehow sticks.

*"God has the heart of a mother. Like a mother, God's love is unconditional. Like a mother, God's forgiveness is complete."*

Although those words must be meant to comfort, they cut me to the core. They burn and sting and taunt. I find it impossible to believe that they are true. And it takes all my self-control not to scream and run out of here. Instead, I dig my fingernails into my palms until I'm sure they must be bleeding.

"Are you okay?" Aunt Kellie looks down at me, and I realize that she and everyone else are standing. My dad is in the aisle talking to Dr. Richards, our dentist. Maybe he's making an appointment for a checkup. Uncle Don has already made his exit.

"Cleo?" My aunt peers curiously at me. "Are you all right?"

"Yeah. Just not feeling too good." I slowly stand, trying to look normal.

She puts her face close to mine. "You don't look too good."

"Thanks," I say with sarcasm.

She links her arm into mine and escorts me down the aisle and toward the door. Once we are out in the parking lot, she gets a somber look. "I'm very concerned about you."

I just shrug, blinking into the sunlight. Then I turn away from her, focusing on a search for my sunglasses in this cavernous bag. I find them and slip them on, hoping this will help to keep her from studying the condition of my pupils again.

"I want to talk to you," she says in a serious tone. Then she looks around, and seeing others coming into the parking lot, she seems to change her mind. "But not here. We'll talk at home."

"Why don't you go home with Uncle Don?"

"Because you need me more than he does right now."

I want to protest this, but my dad is approaching. Like Aunt Kellie, he questions my health, and I assure him I'm fine, just tired. I consider begging out of the cemetery visit, but this will only raise more questions and suspicion. Dad stops by a florist shop, but seeing they're closed, he goes to a grocery store instead.

"I haven't told your dad about Trina's phone call yet," my aunt informs me as we wait for Dad to emerge from the store.

I don't respond.

"He seemed so upset about you last night; I didn't want to add to his stress."

I want to question just how much she added to Dad's stress

in regard to me. Because I'm certain she was the one who planted those ideas in his head last night—suggesting that he'd neglected Mom and me and was somehow responsible for all our problems. It seems like something she would do. But I don't get the chance to say anything because Dad is on his way back to the car.

"No roses." He hands a mixed bouquet to Aunt Kellie. "But these are pretty."

"Yes," she agrees. "These are pretty. And look, there are some tulips in here. You know, Karen loved tulips. Maybe even more than roses. But you can only get tulips in the spring."

I want to yell at her now, to tell her to shut up about the stupid tulips, but somehow I manage to keep my mouth shut. And soon we're at the cemetery. I'm not sure if it's the pills I'm taking or if I'm going insane, but for a while I think it's the day of my mother's funeral. Where is everyone, and why is her grave all covered with dirt and sod now?

I stand about ten feet away from the grave as my dad kneels and lays the flowers by the headstone. He remains there on his knees, and I wonder if he's praying . . . or maybe he's talking to my mother. Is he telling her he's sorry? Telling her that this whole thing, her untimely death, is all his fault?

My dad stands and Aunt Kellie loudly blows her nose in a hankie; I stay rooted to the ground, longing to get away from this place. Without speaking to me, Dad turns and walks away. Then Aunt Kellie follows. And I am left standing here.

I should follow them, but for some reason I feel frozen. And I want to say something—like I almost believe my mom is really here and can actually hear me. Even though I know better.

I open my mouth, but no words come out. Instead I hear this horrible, awful sound—like the howl of a mortally wounded animal. I collapse in tears, dropping to my knees with my face to the ground and falling completely apart.

I'm not sure how long I remain in that position or how my dad and aunt got me to the car. But while I'm in the backseat, crouched in a fetal position, I realize that I'm no longer in the cemetery. I'm still sobbing, but I can hear the sound of voices: my dad in front and my aunt back here. And although I can't make out the words, I suspect they are talking about me, trying to decide how to deal with this. But when I hear my dad mention the hospital, I sit up.

"Don't take me to the hospital!" I shriek.

"But you're so upset," he says. "You need help, Cleo."

"Not the hospital," I plead. "I promise, I'll be okay. Just take me home, and I'll be okay."

"But you're not yourself," my aunt tells me. "Something . . . something beyond losing your mother is wrong."

"How do you know what's wrong? You're not me."

"We can see you, honey," Dad says soothingly. "You are acting very strangely."

I bury my face in my hands and cry uncontrollably again. *I wish I were dead, I wish I were dead, I wish I were dead.*

The next thing I know, I am being helped from the car — but we're not at home. We are at the hospital. With my aunt and my dad on either side of me, supporting me between them, I'm being guided toward a set of doors with a sign that says EMERGENCY above it. Fine. Maybe I am an emergency. Let them see if they can fix me.

It's not until I'm alone in the examining room with the doctor that I consider just telling the truth. Really, it would be simpler. But the doctor, who seems awfully young, also seems busy and distracted, and I suspect he has more urgent patients to attend to, probably with problems more serious than a crazy teenager.

"I understand you're having an extremely difficult time dealing with the loss of your mother," he says quietly. "And I'm no expert in grief, but I do recommend you get into some kind of grief therapy. We have a list of resources."

I just nod, wanting to get this over with. "Thanks. I'll do that."

"Your father is worried that you might want to harm yourself. He said you were saying that you wished you were dead. Is that right?"

I blink. Did I really say that out loud? "I, uh, I don't know. It was just so painful being at my mother's grave . . . I guess I kind of fell apart."

"That must've been rough."

"And it's Mother's Day, you know." I sigh sadly. "I think it was just too much emotion to deal with."

"Well, we don't really have any reason to keep you here." He reads what I assume is my chart. "You were pretty stressed when you got here, but you seem fairly rational now. Grief does strange things to people, but it's not usually a reason to hospitalize someone. So tell me, how are you feeling now?"

"Like I want to go home." I look hopefully at him. "If I can just get some rest, I think I'll be fine. I mean, I haven't really been sleeping that well, you know, since my mom was killed."

"That's understandable, too." He writes something on a prescription pad. "I'll prescribe something to help calm you down." He holds out the paper. "But only if you promise to get yourself into some grief therapy."

"I promise." I nod. "I think that might help."

He hands me the paper and smiles. "Just give yourself time,

Cleo. Some people take more time to get over these things than others. But you're going to be okay."

I want to question this, but at the same time I just want to get out of here. And I cannot believe this clueless MD is actually giving me a prescription for Xanax! Not that I plan to point out his ignorance. And even if I did, I don't get the chance. The doctor is needed in another room where victims of a bad car wreck have just been brought in.

I try to act normal as I go out and rejoin my dad and aunt. They look surprised to see me, but I show them the prescription and explain my promise to get some grief therapy as well as some rest. And amazingly, this seems to do the trick. At least with my dad. My aunt still looks a little skeptical.

"I'll drop you ladies off," Dad says as he pulls into the driveway, "and I'll go fill this prescription."

A part of me wants to tell him to forget it, I don't need more pills, but another part of me is eagerly rubbing her palms together. I don't get me.

I thank Dad, then hurry into the house, but before I make it to my room, Aunt Kellie puts a hand on my shoulder and stops me.

"We need to talk, Cleo." Her voice is very firm.

"I need to sleep."

"You can sleep later," she says a bit more gently. "Right now, we need to talk. Where would you like to talk?"

I shrug.

"Your room?"

"Okay." I continue on to my room, sit on my bed, and wait as she pulls out a chair from my desk and makes herself comfortable.

"I'm fairly certain that you have something you need to tell me," she says with her eyes locked onto my face.

"What do you mean?"

She leans back into the chair, pressing her lips together.

"You're the one who wanted to talk to me," I remind her.

She nods. "That's true. Well, let me tell you a little bit about how I grew up. And how your mom grew up."

She starts talking about her childhood and her dysfunctional family. Some parts sound familiar, like I knew the kids' names all started with K and my mom's parents were a little flaky. But it seems it was worse than that.

"Due to some work injuries, our dad worked off and on, mostly off. And both of our parents drank all the time. When I was ten, our mom left us. Our dad went on a binge that lasted for years." She shakes her head. "Karen—your mom—was only twelve, but she tried to take over as the mom. She used food stamps to get groceries, cooked and cleaned, and tried to keep us kids in line. And it wasn't easy. Kenny was actually a couple years older than Karen, but he didn't spend much time at home. And he dropped out of high school and went to Vietnam when he was seventeen . . . came home in a pine box. That was hard."

She removes a tissue from her pocket, twists it in her hands. "Then there was Kevin. He was two years younger than me. Poor Kevin. He was a sweet kid, but he got involved with a bad bunch. Was hooked on drugs by the time he was fourteen." She pauses, studying me closely. "So don't let my age fool you; I remember what that was like. I remember the ups and downs with him, the moodiness, the tiredness, the anger, the hopelessness. He was my favorite brother, and I still remember that look in his eyes and the way his pupils would change—from big to pinpoints. There was even a smell about him." She sighs sadly.

"It's all painfully familiar to me. Some things you never forget."

I look down at my hands in my lap. They are trembling, and I'm longing for a pain pill . . . or that Xanax my dad is picking up for me. Anything to block all this out.

"I don't like to point fingers or make false accusations, Cleo, but I'm pretty sure you've been using something, too. The signs are all there."

I still don't respond, but I feel like my insides are shaking now, like the truth is written all over my face.

"During my senior year, Kevin died of a heroin overdose," she says quietly. "He was only sixteen. Just a little younger than you."

She's trying to shock me with this little history lesson, and I must admit that she's gotten my attention, but I'm determined to keep my emotional distance. I will remain aloof.

"Did your mother ever tell you about any of this?"

I barely look up, barely shake my head. "Not really."

"No, I didn't think so."

For some reason this intrigues me. "Why not?"

She shrugs. "I think she wanted to protect you from all that. She wanted your world—and her world—to be perfect and safe and lovely. Nothing like the world she grew up in."

"Yeah . . . I guess I kind of knew that." A lump is growing in my throat. It hurts to think of my mother like that, imagining the messed-up family she came from and how hard she worked to hide it from me, to protect me.

"And then there was Special K," Aunt Kellie says wistfully.

"Huh?"

"Your mother never told you about Special K?"

I frown. "The cereal?"

"No. Our youngest brother, Kyle. He was only four when

our mom abandoned us. Kyle was a sweetheart, but he had Down syndrome. He was in special-ed classes, so we called him Special K. I guess that's not very politically correct, but he liked the name and we meant no harm."

"Special K?" I try out the name. "Where is he?"

"He passed on too. Although of all my brothers, Special K had the best life. He went into foster care in grade school, then got adopted by a real nice family. As an adult, he lived in a sort of halfway house. He passed on a couple years before you were born. Your mother used to visit him all the time. She'd take him places and buy him things. Sometimes I wonder if that wasn't the reason she finally decided to have a baby."

"Why?"

"Because after Special K was gone, she needed someone to need her like he had." Aunt Kellie shrugs. "But I could be wrong."

"I know she hadn't really planned to have kids. She waited a long time to have me."

"And you were the happiest thing in her life, Cleo. Did you know that?"

I look back down at my lap, but my vision is blurred by my tears. The ache inside me feels unbearable, like I'm being pulled so hard from side to side that I'll split right down the middle. I want to tell the truth, I want to confess everything I've done wrong . . . but if I do this, I will lose everything.

"You can talk to me, Cleo. There's not much I haven't heard or seen in this world. I seriously doubt there's anything you can tell me that would shock me."

I look at her with teary eyes. *"Really? Nothing?"*

"I don't think so."

I don't believe her. I'm certain she would be horrified to

know that I'm the one who's responsible for her sister's death. To learn that I'm as guilty as the low-life drug-addict murderer would surely rock her world. *That* would shock her.

My aunt is just about to give up on me when my dad knocks on the door. "I have your prescription," he says as she opens it. "Oh?" He looks curiously at her. "What are you doing in here?"

"We were talking." Aunt Kellie points to the bag in his hand. "I think maybe I should keep that for Cleo."

Dad looks confused, and I don't know what to say. But my aunt doesn't seem to budge as she holds out her hand for the little white bag.

"Why?" Dad asks her. "Shouldn't Cleo take care of this herself?"

Aunt Kellie turns to look at me. "What do you think, Cleo?"

"I . . . uh . . . I don't know."

"I just think we want to be safe," my aunt says. "Cleo hasn't really been herself lately, and I'm worried she might forget and accidentally take too many of these pills, Hugh. That could be very dangerous."

His brows arch and he nods. "You're right, Kellie." He seems relieved to hand her the bag. "I'd appreciate your help with this."

"And while we're all together, there's something we need to

tell you about," she continues.

Suddenly I feel certain she's going to expose me by sharing her suspicions about my recently acquired drug habit, but instead she explains that there's a phone message he needs to hear.

"A phone message?" He frowns. "Is it from the police? Have they found the murderer?"

"No, but it might be something the police would be interested in. I saved it for you."

I wish I'd had the foresight to erase Trina's message. How easy would that have been? Of course, my aunt would probably just call Trina, and then I'd have to explain how the message was deleted and I'd be buried even deeper in my mire of lies.

I listen as my dad and aunt go down the hallway. When they're a safe distance away, I get into my secret stash, pull out a pain pill, and pop it into my mouth, swallowing it dry. Then I hurry to where they're both standing by the answering machine as my dad searches for Trina's message.

Finally it's playing, and I hang in the shadows, listening to the words again. Then after Dad hits Replay, I hear it for the third time. And it sounds even more suspicious.

"That's so strange," Dad says as he picks up the phone. "It just doesn't make sense. I'm going to call Trina right now and see if I can get to the bottom of this. Maybe that woman is delusional."

I listen as Dad leaves a message for Trina, but I'm relieved that she's not around to fill in any more blanks. Dad turns to me as soon as he hangs up. "Did your mother call you that night, Cleo? The night she went to Trina's party? Did she call to check up on you or anything?"

"I . . . uh . . . I can't remember exactly."

"You *can't* remember?" He stares at me like he questions my sensibility. "The night your mother was murdered, and you can't remember?"

"Well, it was Lola's last night here. She and her family were moving the very next day. So I was at her house for a while, and I'd told Mom I was sleeping over there, but then Lola decided we should spend the night here because her house was pretty much a wasteland by then." I frown like I'm trying to remember the evening correctly, but I'm really trying not to say too much.

I've decided that the trick with lying is to leave out details, keep it simple, don't say too much. The problem is that when I get caught — and it feels like that moment is getting closer — anything and everything I say will be used against me.

"So did your mother call your cell phone?"

"My cell phone was dead that night."

"Did she call the house?"

"I don't think so. Lola and I watched a movie and fell asleep. Later on, I figured Mom had come home while we were asleep, but then she was gone the next morning, and I assumed she'd gone out or something." At least that much is true.

"And your mom didn't leave a message anywhere?"

"I don't think so."

"Don't the police have her cell phone?" Aunt Kellie says suddenly. "That would show what calls were made. Or the phone company records, they would show when any calls were placed."

Dad nods. "That's true. Tomorrow I'll check with the police. I should probably see about picking her car up, too." He looks at me. "Do you still think you want it?"

I take in a shaky breath. "I . . . uh . . . I don't know."

"I keep thinking this will all finally come to an end," Dad

says sadly, "and then maybe we'll be able to move on with our lives. But I suppose that until the murderer is taken into custody . . . or maybe until after the trial is over . . . then we'll still have to keep dealing with — with all of it."

I feel sick now. Like I'm really about to throw up. I hurry away, going into the bathroom and locking the door. I sink onto the tile floor in front of the toilet and just cry. I want this to end, too. I want it all to end. The pain, the lies, the sadness — why can't it just go away? And if it won't go away, if I'll never be free of all this, why should I go on living? What does my life consist of anyway? Endless nameless pills? Feeling out of control, teetering on the edge? Creepy drug deals with T. J.? Hiding, lying, wishing I were dead? What's the point?

A tapping on the door brings me back to reality. My twisted reality.

My aunt calls my name, asking if I'm all right.

"I'm fine," I say grumpily, using the edge of the bathtub to push myself to my feet. "Just peachy." I unlock the door and emerge. "There." I attempt to move past her bulky form. "The bathroom's all yours."

"Not so quick." With highly arched brows, she holds out the slightly dog-eared tampon box in front of me. "Care to explain this?"

"In my room," I say quietly as I hurry past her, waiting until she joins me, then I close the door. "Why are you snooping through my things?"

"I simply came in here to look for you. I saw the box on your bed and realized you were in the bathroom. I thought perhaps you needed this. I mean, you've been pretty moody; I thought maybe it was that time of the month . . ."

"Oh." I snatch the box from her. "Thanks."

She just stands there looking at me, as if she expects me to say something more. My eyes are on the contents of the box, and I want to check to see if the pills are still there. But she holds up her other hand, and in it is the Ziploc bag and what's left of my recently purchased pill supply. "Can we talk now?" she asks gently.

I sink onto the edge of my bed, my arms and legs drooping like a puppet whose strings have been snipped. I am so tired. Too tired to fight this anymore.

"I was right. You have been using drugs."

Without looking up, I just nod.

"Can I ask when you started doing this, Cleo? Will you give me an honest answer?"

"After Mom died."

She doesn't say anything. And when I look up, she has tears in her eyes.

"I needed them, Aunt Kellie. I couldn't function. I was in so much pain . . . and I found some old pain pills that Mom hadn't used. I tried one, and I felt better."

"So you continued to use them?" she asks. I nod. "And then you ran out?"

"I wasn't sleeping at night. And then I could barely stay awake at school. A guy there told me about someone who could get them for me."

She holds up the baggie. "Do you even know what these are, Cleo?"

"Not exactly. Not by name anyway. But I know which ones to take when I need them. And really, isn't that what people do? What about the doctor in the ER today? Even he prescribed pills to help me."

She sighs. "That was unfortunate, or maybe a blessing in

disguise because it's helped to bring the truth to light."

"The truth . . ." I shake my head.

"There's more to the truth, isn't there, Cleo?"

I give her my best innocent look. "What do you mean?"

"I mean something is eating away at you. It has since the day your mother died. I suspect you feel guilty about something. And feeling guilty after a loved one dies is perfectly normal. Take it from me, I know." Then she tells me about how she felt guilty when Kenny died in Vietnam, how she knew if she'd written him more letters, encouraged him more, he would've tried harder to come home. "And then there was Kevin." She's crying now. "If I'd been more involved with him . . . if I'd tried to get him away from his bad friends . . . or maybe even if I told someone when I knew he was doing drugs, maybe he'd still be alive."

"But he made his own choices, Aunt Kellie. Both your brothers did."

"And so did your mother."

I'm trying to wrap my head around this.

"For some reason your mother chose to go to the city that night. You didn't choose for her, did you?"

"No . . . but—"

"Don't get me wrong; I have a strong suspicion her reason for going to the city that night was related to you. But did you make the choice for her to go there?"

I'm just staring at my aunt now, no longer seeing her as an old-fashioned dim-witted frump but as a person with far more sense than I imagined possible.

"Did you?"

"No," I say quietly.

"So . . . why don't you tell me what really happened that night?"

The lump in my throat is getting big again; the tears are stinging behind my eyelids. "I—uh—I don't think I can," I gasp.

Now she sits beside me on my bed, wrapping an arm around me and pulling me close. "Cleo, your mother loved you more than anything in this world. More than she loved Hugh or herself. More than anyone. Do you believe that?"

I just nod, but the tears are streaking down both cheeks.

"Your mother would've done anything for you. And there is absolutely nothing you can do, nothing you could've done, that your mother wouldn't forgive you for. It's like your pastor said today. God is like a very good mother who loves you no matter what and forgives you for anything. Now, I wasn't blessed to have a mother like that myself. Neither was Karen. But she did everything she knew how to become a mother like that. And sure, maybe she took it too far at times. But it was only because she loved you so much."

"I—I know," I sob.

Aunt Kellie hands me a tissue. "Now, tell me what happened, Cleo. And know that you can trust me—just as much as you could trust your mother. Okay?"

"Okay . . ." And after I stop crying, after I'm able to breathe without choking, I spill out the whole horrible, sordid story. And Aunt Kellie just listens. She doesn't act shocked. Doesn't show disapproval. She simply listens. And when I'm done, she hugs me tight, stroking my hair, and promises me that it's going to be okay.

"Things are going to get better, Cleo."

"I *want* to believe that."

"They will. I promise you, they will. But first we need to tell your dad."

I take in a shaky breath. "I'm not sure that I can."

"You can do this, Cleo." She takes my hand. "I'll help you."

I feel like some of the load has been lifted from me, and that's reassuring. But the idea of telling my dad what I just told Aunt Kellie feels like jumping off a cliff. On one hand, it might end this thing. On the other hand, it might hurt an awful lot when I land.

By the time I finish telling my dad the truth, he looks like I just aimed a gun at him and shot him in the chest. But instead of crying out in pain, collapsing on the kitchen floor, and bleeding to death, he turns from me, walks out of the house, gets in his car, and drives away.

I look at Aunt Kellie, and she simply shakes her head. "Give him some time, Cleo."

"But you were so understanding. Why didn't Dad—?"

"I should've considered the shock factor for him. Remember, I already had my suspicions regarding all this. But your father probably felt completely blindsided by it. The perfect image of his perfect little princess was just shattered for him."

"But you told me to confess—"

"You did the right thing, Cleo. And your dad will come around in time."

"But what if he doesn't?"

"If he's the man your mother believed him to be, he will. He just needs some time to sort these things out. He's been through a lot this past month. We all have."

I go over and hug her. "Thanks for standing by me." Fresh tears are coming now. "And I'm sorry for all I put you through.

I can't believe what a spoiled brat I've been to you the past few weeks. And you were just trying to help me. You must've thought I was horrible."

"Like I told you, there's not much you could do or say that would shock or disappoint me. I've pretty much seen it all. I knew you were going through something beyond your mother's death. I'm just glad you finally got it out in the open."

"I don't know if Dad is ever going to feel that way." I take a paper napkin from the basket and wipe my tears with it. "What if he never forgives me?"

"You can't control his response, Cleo. It's his choice whether or not to forgive. Just like it was your mom's choice whether or not to go into the city that night. You can't take responsibility for either of those choices."

"No, but I can suffer the consequences."

"That's true. You can also prolong the suffering if you refuse to forgive yourself."

"It'd be a whole lot easier to forgive myself if I knew that my dad was going to forgive me, too."

"Time will tell."

I'm pacing in the kitchen now, feeling—more than ever—the need for another pill, some kind of relief. Aunt Kellie is calmly putting on the teakettle, like she doesn't have a care in the world.

"I don't know if I can do this," I say suddenly.

She turns, looks at me. "Do what?"

"Make it—without pills."

"Oh . . ." She opens the cupboard and gets out a box of chamomile tea.

"What if I just have one of the prescription pills—you know, the ones the ER doctor prescribed?"

"When did you last take a pill, Cleo?"

"I don't know."

"Think hard. When did you last have one?" She looks evenly at me, and I can tell she already knows the answer.

"Right before Dad checked the answering machine," I confess.

"And what kind of pill did you have?"

I think hard. "A pain pill."

"And before that pill? What did you take?"

"That was this morning. I took one of the amphetamines. Just one."

"And before that?"

I'm pacing again, trying to remember, trying to be honest. "Last night, really late, I took a sleeping pill. I'd already taken one, but I needed two last night."

"I'm not saying this is going to be easy, Cleo, but I think now that you've told the truth, you won't need the pills like you did before."

"But I need one now!"

"Yes. Your body is telling you it needs one. But what does your mind say? What does your heart tell you?"

I sit down, trying to think about this. What does my mind say? And my heart? I remember how many times I've hated myself for needing chemicals like this. Now I have the chance to stop this madness. "Do you think I'm an addict? I mean, a serious addict?"

She smiles. "I think you were on the way to becoming one. And your body has become dependent on drugs. But with some help, you can beat this."

The teakettle whistles, and she pours the hot water into one of my mother's favorite teapots, and the smell of chamomile tea wafts through the kitchen. "I know this isn't as strong as what you've been using" — she slides a cup toward me — "but it might help."

As we sip our tea, I tell her a bit more about how hard it's been these past few weeks, tell her what a relief it is to have the truth out in the open. "Except for that look on my dad's face. That was awful."

She nods. "Yes. I know."

"And really, I'm not sure I can forgive myself, even if Dad forgives me. I mean, I will always know that Mom went there that night because of me. Because I went to the city even though she told me not to. I'll always know that if not for me, she would still be alive. That feels like it's my fault."

Aunt Kellie sits across from me. Her eyes are sad, and she's looking over her cup of tea and out the window, as if she's seeing something else besides the cherry tree in our backyard and the grass that needs mowing. "We can blame ourselves for things that were beyond our control for a lifetime, Cleo. We can torture ourselves for years and years. But someday, we have to accept that we don't control anyone but ourselves. And then we have to account for all the time we lost fretting over those things we couldn't control."

"Like blaming yourself for the deaths of your brothers?"

She nods. "And other things."

"Like what?"

"There's something I never told anyone, Cleo. Well, besides God, and it took me far too long to do that."

"What is it? Will you tell me?"

"I think I will. But only because of what you confessed to me today." Her eyes are misty now. "It happened one morning when I was ten and fed up with the way my family lived. I was late for school — and I knew I'd get detention for it — but the dress I wanted to wear was still in the washing machine, along with the other clothes I had put in there to wash the day before. Really, it was my own fault that it never made it to the dryer. I mean, we'd been doing our own laundry for years by then. But my mother was in the kitchen, and I yelled at her and told her it was her fault that I was going to have detention. I told her she was the worst mother in the world and that we would all be better off without her." Aunt Kellie lets out a little sob. "And really, it was kind of true. But it was cruel and selfish. And that was the day . . ."

"The day she left?"

Aunt Kellie just nods. "I never told any of my siblings. Not even Karen, and I told her almost everything."

"Oh . . ."

"So you see, I really did feel as if I were to blame for all that my siblings suffered in the following years."

"But like you said, you didn't control your mom's decision to leave, right?"

"That's right. But in my heart, I felt that I did. It took me years to figure it out. And as you can see, it still hurts now."

"But lots of kids tell their moms things like that. I've heard Lola telling her mom off lots of times."

"But Lola's mother didn't leave and never come back."

"No. Well, she left, but she took Lola with her."

"The only reason I told you is because I thought you would understand, Cleo."

"I do understand." I reach out and place my hand over hers.

"I carried that guilt far into adulthood and into my marriage, too. And it's why I never had children. In fact, long ago your mother and I made a pact never to have children."

"A pact?"

"It's sad, but true. I think we were partly worried we'd have children as messed up as our parents . . . or even like some of our brothers. But that wasn't all. We were equally worried that we would repeat history and fail as mothers."

"My mother was a fantastic mom," I assure her. "And you would be too."

She smiles sadly. "Thanks. And I know your mother was proud of you. How many times did she whisper to me, at one of your recitals or some other event, that you'd come out all right?"

"Until recently."

"But you're turning it around now. You're going to learn from this. And you'll be stronger for it. You won't let it ruin your life. It's not going to define who you are, Cleo. You are going to make your mother proud."

"And my father?"

"He'll be proud, too. In time, he'll be proud. In the meantime, you need to remember that you have another father, a powerful heavenly father, who loves you even more fiercely than your mother ever could."

"I haven't been able to pray . . . not since she died."

"But now you've confessed your sin to me, Cleo. And you need to confess it to God, too. Pour out your heart to him. He'll forgive you and cleanse you. And he'll give you a fresh start."

She offers to pray with me, and we bow our heads right there in the kitchen. And I confess all that I've messed up to God. I even tell him about how I was so angry at him, how I blamed him, turned my back on him, even though I knew it was my own selfish fault that I was so miserable. By the time we say "amen," I do feel different. And I feel like God's forgiven me.

As for my dad . . . I don't know.

· · · · · · · ·

Not only does my father not offer any forgiveness, he is not speaking to me either. He leaves for his next trip without saying a word, not even good-bye. But somehow, even without pills, I survive the next few days. This is mostly due to Aunt Kellie.

First she takes away my cell phone, and then she keeps her promise—she stands by me as I experience withdrawal. Actually she spends more time sitting with me. She sits by my bed as I experience chills and fever and shaking. And when I start crying and can't stop, she holds my hand. Then she holds my hair away from my face as I barf my guts out into the toilet.

By Wednesday afternoon, the physical symptoms subside some. Except for the shaking—that still comes and goes. But now I am so conscious, so aware, so raw—all I want is something to take the edge off . . . a little relief.

But when Aunt Kellie catches me with my hand on the phone (I don't think I really planned to call T. J., but I'm not totally sure either), she removes the phone from the jack and hands me a notebook and a pen.

"Write about your feelings," she instructs me. "It's good therapy." Then she takes me into the kitchen, where she makes me chamomile tea and toast. "Things are getting better, Cleo, and you're doing great."

And then she puts her hands on my head and prays for me to be healed. This is something new to me, but it feels amazingly good and it gives me hope.

I write out my thoughts and my fears and my feelings, filling up page after page of my journal—most of it's about Mom. And Aunt Kellie keeps on cooking things she thinks I'll want to eat. Sometimes she reads to me from her Bible. And she prays with me. This continues for three days. Three long days.

"I thought going through all that, you know, losing Mom and everything . . . was the hardest thing I'd ever go through," I tell Aunt Kellie on Saturday evening as I'm getting ready for bed. We think that Monday I should return to school. "And it really was . . . actually it still is. But I think the past three days might've been the hardest part yet."

"You know, Jesus spent three days in the grave," she tells me as she brushes my hair. "And then he rose from the dead."

"Do you think I can do that?" I sigh. "Rise from the dead?"

"All things are possible with God."

I know what I'm experiencing is a relatively small form of withdrawal. Because my aunt tells me about others she's known who went through some major withdrawal from extremely addictive substances like cocaine or methamphetamines. Even so, this feels hard enough for me, and I'm thankful I wasn't even more addicted to those stupid pills. And now when I say, "Never again," I'm pretty sure I mean it. Just the idea of chills, fever, shaking, and vomiting makes me want to stay far, far away from that crud.

As Aunt Kellie drives me to school on Monday, I feel like I've climbed a mountain. Even though I still feel a little shaky around the edges, I'm ready to return to my former life. But I never could've done it without Aunt Kellie and God, plus my journal and a couple of very honest phone calls with my old friend Lola, who now knows the whole story.

"I can't believe everything you've gone through," Lola told me last night. "I wish I'd been there for you. I mean, I was actually feeling sorry for myself because I was having a hard time restarting my life without my best friend by my side. I can't even imagine how you're doing it—especially with all the crud you've been hit with. I think I'd have been totally devastated."

"I was devastated," I admitted. "But I've been learning how to rely on God more."

"That's great to hear. You have no idea how much I've been praying for you, Cleo."

"I can tell." And then I asked her to pray for my first day back at school — drug free. "I know it's going to be hard."

"You're going to do fine," she assured me with far more confidence than I could muster. "I just know. And trust me, I'll be praying!"

By the end of the school day, I feel certain that she was praying. Not only that, I almost feel like I'm becoming myself again. Okay, a different kind of myself. Or maybe I'm just becoming more of a complete person.

Daniel and the others show me sympathy, thinking that I've been home with a bad case of flu. And part of me wants to tell them the truth, but the rest of me isn't ready for that just yet. So I suppose I might seem a bit distant . . . disconnected. But I'm doing the best I can.

Amanda isn't a bit happy to see me back at ballet. In fact, she actually thought I'd quit for good. But I'm more determined than ever to do my very best in the recital — without pills. So unless I break a leg, literally, I will be dancing the lead. Not only do I want to make my mom proud, but Madame Reginald as well. Especially after she's been so understanding.

"You've been different today," Daniel tells me on Thursday when he meets me after ballet and, as usual, we get coffee. "You seem quieter."

It's funny because something about being in school, dancing in ballet, standing up to Amanda, and keeping my promise to Madame makes me feel stronger somehow. I think I'm ready to tell him the truth.

"Yeah," I say slowly. "In fact, there's something I've been wanting to explain to you." I feel nervous and yet strangely calm at the same time. I want to confess to Daniel about what I've gone through, starting with the night my mom was murdered until now.

This could end our relationship, but I'm so tired of lies that I'm willing to take the risk. I just want to be free of all this—as free as I can be anyway. Not only do I admit to him that I blamed myself for Mom's death, but I also confess how that guilt pushed me to use drugs.

"It's humiliating to tell you this," I say finally. "But if we're going to be together, you deserve to know the truth about me."

"Wow." He slowly shakes his head with a stunned expression. "Wow . . ."

"I know, it's pretty creepy. And I realize that this might change how you feel about me. I mean, in a way, I deceived you too. I deceived everyone. Mostly myself. And as hard as it is to admit what I did—especially to say those words out loud—it's a huge relief to have it out in the open." Maybe the truth really does set you free.

To my surprise, he chuckles. "It's funny, you know, because Geoff made a comment after that night we went to the movies. The next day, he texted me saying he suspected you were high on something. But I texted him back, saying he was nuts and you would never use drugs."

"But he was absolutely right."

"Are you going to tell him, too?"

I shrug. "I don't see why he needs to know everything. Not that I want to hide it. And I don't mind if you tell him. It's up to you, Daniel."

"I don't see why he needs to know either."

"And really, I'll understand if you don't want to be with me now."

He laughs. "Are you kidding?"

"No." I stare at him in wonder. Is this even possible? Does Daniel still like me?

"So are you saying you don't want to be *with me* now?" He looks slightly worried.

"Of course not." I can't help but smile at him. I had so hoped this would be his reaction, but I was prepared for the worst. And I told myself that if he wasn't who I thought he was, I'd be better off without him anyway. Still I'm relieved.

"It's good to see you happier, Cleo."

"It's weird. I *do* feel happier. Not exactly happy-happy. I mean, in some ways it feels like I'm still in the early stages of the grief process. But according to the book I'm reading, that's normal. When you use something to block your emotions, it's like you get stuck. It's better to just experience the pain . . . deal with it . . . get beyond it."

"Are you going to that grief group?"

I nod. "I'll be there. Saturday morning."

"And my offer's still good. I'll go with you if you want."

"I appreciate that. But I'm okay to go on my own. Unless you want to go for your own sake."

"No, I'm pretty much okay."

We talk some more, and as he drives me home, I feel like life is on its way back to some kind of normal. And that actually feels pretty good. Like I might have a life again. An authentic life where I face even the hardest kind of truth and don't use chemicals to escape. And sure, it's a challenge, but the reward — a deep sense of peace and wholeness — seems to be worth it.

By the weekend, and after my first experience with the grief group, I feel even more hopeful. I think I'm starting to heal, and the pieces are slowly being put back together again. However, there's one part of my life that's still broken.

My dad is still angry at me.

He's home from his trip now, and I'm trying to stay out of his way, mostly in my room, since my very presence seems to aggravate him even more. On Sunday night, he made an excuse to take his dinner to his office, claiming he would work while he ate. But I know he's just trying to avoid me. And that hurts a lot.

I even wrote out a long letter of apology to him last night. I left it on his desk this morning before church, which he also "excused" himself from. I have no idea whether or not he's read my letter . . . or if he'll respond. And really, I can't blame him. How do you forgive someone for being part of the reason that the love of your life is gone?

Just thinking of this still slices me to the core. I realize my mom made her own choice that night. I can accept that I had no control over that. But at the same time, I'm fully aware that if I hadn't disobeyed her wishes for me to stay home, she never would've made that choice.

"I know your mom was having a hard time letting you grow up," Aunt Kellie tells me as I help her clean up after dinner. As it often happens now, our conversation drifts toward my mom. It's like I'm still processing a lot of things. "And I'm sure most other girls your age would've been allowed to do things that Karen wasn't comfortable with."

"That's true." I nod. "Lola's mom pretty much lets her do as she pleases. Her theory is that Lola's going to make mistakes, and she'd rather she made them while she's living at home than when she's off at college."

"That seems sensible. But in your mom's defense, she was like a pendulum."

"Pendulum?" I pause from rinsing a plate.

"You know how you swing a pendulum one way and it naturally has to swing back to the opposite side?"

"Yeah."

"Well, your mom was swinging in the opposite direction of her upbringing. Our parents failed miserably at protecting their children. Your mom was determined to protect you from everything and anything. As negligent as our parents were, your mom was kind of obsessed with your safety and well-being."

"I know."

"I remember talking to her a few months ago. I asked her how she was going to do when you went away to college." Aunt Kellie sighed and shook her head. "It seemed like she didn't even want to think about it."

"She never wanted to *talk* about it either. It's like she was in denial, like she honestly believed that I was never going to leave this home."

"It would've been hard on her."

"And me too," I admit. "Now it's like it can't happen soon enough."

"What do you mean?"

"I'm sure that Dad can't wait until I'm gone." I start feeling weepy now. But I know that's normal, and I need to let the tears fall. I need to feel this pain; it's the only way to get better.

"He's going to come around, Cleo." Aunt Kellie hands me a paper towel for my nose and gives me a hug. "You just need to be patient."

"Yeah . . . I know." And I'm trying to be patient, but I'm worried that he's never going to get past this thing—he's never going to forgive me. I've heard of people who carry a grudge for years, getting more and more bitter and closed off. I hate to think of that happening to my dad. Not just in regard to my relationship with him, but I hate to think of him being so miserable with others as well. For his own sake, I wish he could forgive me . . . move on.

But the fact that he's still avoiding me and planning to leave for another business trip tomorrow — not that I blame him — sends a pretty clear message that he wants to keep distancing himself from me. Even so, I'm praying I'll get the chance to speak to him before he leaves. Another week of being cut off like this feels unendurable.

## CHAPTER 20

**W**eek two of my "recovery program" begins with my father slipping off to the airport without saying a word to me. Granted, his flight was very early Monday, and I could tell myself he didn't want to disturb my sleep, except that I know better.

Aunt Kellie keeps saying, "Just give him time . . . he'll come around." And I assure her I will do that. My question is, How much time? Will he come around by the time I leave for college? Get married? Have children? Grow old? Die?

The grief group continues to be a pretty good thing. But after Saturday's session ends, an older woman named Margie approaches me, encouraging me to have a "conversation" with my mom. Naturally, I feel skeptical.

"It made a big difference in my own recovery," she explains with a wide-eyed intensity that scares me a little. "Once I sat down and just talked openly with Kristen, I started to find some closure."

Now I know that Kristen is her deceased daughter. In her thirties, she was tragically killed in a car wreck that involved a teen who was texting and driving. But this idea of actually speaking with the dead is hard for me to grasp. And I'm pretty sure that séances are not acceptable in most Christian circles. And it's especially disturbing when Margie makes it sound as if Kristen is actually engaged in the conversation.

"So . . . how do you do that exactly?" I ask out of cynical curiosity. Is this woman for real or just desperately imagining things?

"Well, it involves timing. You can't just force it to happen."

"And you actually *heard* your daughter speaking to you?" I question. "Audibly?"

She laughs. "No, no, it's not like that at all, dear. Forgive me if I made it sound weird. It's just that the experience felt so very real to me, and the impression I got of hearing her" — she pauses to tap her chest — "in here, inside me, was so incredible and genuine. I just knew it was Kristen. But no, I didn't hear her audibly speaking to me. I guess you could call it more of an impression. A bit like the way you feel sometimes when God communicates something to your heart. Does that make sense?"

I nod. "I guess so. But maybe I'm worried about what my mother would say to me. I mean, she was trying to help me when she was murdered. What if she partially blames me for her death?"

Margie seems to consider this. "You have to remember she's on the other side now. She sees things in a more complete sort of way. I know you believe in God, Cleo. Do you believe in heaven, too?"

"I guess so. I mean, I want to believe in heaven, especially for my mom's sake. But it's kind of mind-boggling."

She smiles. "Yes, it's boggled my mind too. But there are a lot of things about God that are difficult to comprehend."

"That's true."

"All I'm saying is you should be open. And pray about it. I

feel sure that eventually you'll get that opportunity to converse with your mother. I'll be praying for that for you, too."

I want to be open to that, but as Aunt Kellie drives me home on Saturday, I'm more concerned about having a conversation with my dad. He got home from his trip very late last night. I still haven't seen him. But because I sneaked into his office and checked his calendar this morning, I also know he leaves for another trip tomorrow evening. This time it's Michigan for two weeks. That doesn't leave a whole lot of time to snag a conversation with him. But he must've read my letter by now. I'm surprised he hasn't at least responded to it. Even if he's still mad, it seems like he'd say *something*. Or maybe he didn't want to read it. Maybe he threw it away.

"Your dad picked up your mom's car this morning," Aunt Kellie tells me in a slightly sober tone. "He brought it home just before I left the house, and it looks like it's in good shape. He must've run it through a carwash or something."

"Oh . . . I thought maybe he'd decided against it."

"Apparently not. And he dropped the car keys on the kitchen counter and said to see that you got them."

"So he's letting me use her car?"

She just nodded.

"I'm not even sure I can do that now."

"Your mother would *want* you to have her car, Cleo. She loved that car, and she was always telling me how safe it is. And I took a peek inside it, and it's just as clean and neat inside as outside. But then it was always like that, wasn't it?" She shakes her head as she glances at the messy interior of her own vehicle. "For sisters, Karen and I were as different as they come."

"But you both have some nice qualities that are similar."

She smiles. "I hope so."

"I'm worried that Dad is never going to forgive me," I quietly admit to her as she turns down our street.

"He certainly is taking his time."

"Tell me about it."

She chuckles. "It reminds me of when he and your mother were courting. We thought he was *never* going to pop the question. But you have to give it to him; once he makes up his mind, he usually sticks to it."

"I just hope he hasn't made up his mind to be angry at me forever."

"I don't think that's going to happen."

*"Oh!"* I let out a little gasp when I see Mom's car parked in the driveway. It's almost as if she's come home . . . although I know that's not possible. As my aunt parks in front of the house, I feel a clutch in my chest, like my heart physically hurts to know that car was the last place Mom was before her death.

"I know," Aunt Kellie says quietly. "I felt the same way when I first saw it."

I get out and cautiously walk around Mom's car, just staring at it like I think it's a living thing about to speak to me, to tell me some secret. I briefly consider Margie's suggestion that I have a conversation with my mother, but I don't think I can get inside of that car to do it. Not right now anyway. Maybe never. Besides, even if I could communicate with her, I'm not sure I'm ready to hear what she might have to say.

· · · · · · · · · ·

To my dismay, my father left for his next trip without saying a word to me. Aunt Kellie was a bit perturbed at him, too. He didn't even tell her good-bye either. Instead, he snuck out while she and I were at church, simply leaving a note that said he drove himself to the airport early and planned to work there until his flight left this evening.

"Don't you think that's a little weird?" I ask her as she makes us some tea. "It seems like a lot of effort to take just to avoid your own daughter."

"Your father has always enjoyed traveling and airports. He's told me more than once that he finds all that hubbub soothing."

Even so, I feel my fate is sealed. I am certain my father is permanently disowning me. Of course, Aunt Kellie keeps telling me that it's just going to take time and that I don't want to rush things with him. "He'll come around when he's ready to come around."

"You know, Lola's been talking about getting a job this summer. She even suggested that I come out to San Diego and get a job too, and we could rent a small apartment together."

"Why would you want to do that?" Aunt Kellie sets her mug of tea down with a clank. "What about college?"

"I'm not giving up on college. But I'm not looking forward to a whole summer of Dad hating me."

"He doesn't hate you, Cleo. He's just confused and upset."

"And you can't stay here forever. What about Uncle Don? Doesn't he miss you?"

She just laughs.

But I realize I might need to start making an escape plan. At the very least, I should find a job for the summer. And it actually sounds fun to me. My mother never let me work before. But not only could I use the job experience, after my recent stupid spree, my savings account could use some replenishing. I still can't believe how much money I wasted on those horrible pills. I must've been truly insane.

· · · · · · · · · ·

As the week passes, my time is consumed with a number of things, including bringing my grades back up so I can graduate with a decent grade-point average. Although some of my teachers cut me some slack, my studies were neglected during my addiction era, and it's up to me to make it right. I've also been madly practicing for the ballet recital, determined to show everyone that Madame didn't make a mistake in choosing me for the lead. I'm also continuing with the grief group, spending time with Daniel, and lately I'm trying to convince Aunt Kellie it's time for her to go home to Uncle Don. I even started driving my mom's car, which was weird at first, but I wanted to show my aunt that I'm becoming more and more independent.

It seems that all this activity would be a great way to block out troublesome thoughts of my father and the silent treatment he's been giving me. Unfortunately, it's not. But instead of obsessing over it, I recently decided to just pray for him whenever I start feeling bad about the whole thing. Only now that I know he'll be home in a few days, it's hard not to start freaking out. And I'm still considering Lola's suggestion about San Diego.

"I just want to stay with you until your graduation," Aunt Kellie tells me as we're cleaning up after dinner on Thursday. Feeling guilty that I've monopolized so much of her time these past several weeks, I've been urging her to return to her own life and husband. "It's the least I can do for Karen," she tells me as she closes the dishwasher. "And the truth is, it's been good medicine for me, too."

"How's that?" I hang the dishtowel on the refrigerator handle, then study my aunt. I've decided that she's actually rather attractive for an older lady. Pleasantly plump, with sparkling brown eyes that remind me of Mom, she's really quite nice-looking. Although she does need fashion direction, which I've been attempting to help her with recently.

"Talking about things with you has been very therapeutic for me."

"Well, I don't think I could've survived all this without you," I confess. "I'm sure I'll never think of a way to appropriately thank you."

"You thank me every day, just by doing what you need to be doing. You've really grown up a lot, Cleo. Your mother would be very proud of you."

A lump grows in my throat now. "Saturday night . . . it's the recital," I say with a raspy voice. "I just can't believe she won't be there. It meant everything to her."

Aunt Kellie puts a hand on my shoulder. "She'll be there."

I nod, pressing my lips together. I want to point out that my father won't be there either, but if I say those words out loud, I don't think I can hold back the tears.

·  ·  ·  ·  ·  ·  ·  ·  ·  ·

With the upcoming recital as motivation, I go to the basement and practice for nearly two hours. Working hard (and without the chemical influence of pills), I dance until my thighs and calves are screaming for a break, and then I flop down on the old pink couch. I can't believe how much I love this couch. In fact, I've decided that if I ever do move out on my own, I'm taking this couch with me. I can't explain why exactly, but more than anything else in the house, this particular piece of furniture reminds me of Mom.

As I sit here, running my hands back and forth over the nap

of the fabric, I feel tears coming. And I know I need to just let them come. "Tears bring healing," the group therapist is always telling us. "Let them flow, and they will cleanse you." And so I do.

Then just as I'm blotting my tears with a tissue, I suddenly hear her speaking to me. Not audibly, of course, but I get the strongest sense that it's Mom I am hearing. Almost afraid to breathe, I lean back into the soft velvet cushions, close my eyes, and just listen.

*You are my treasure.* That's what she just said—I know it! *You are my treasure, Cleo.* It's something she used to say to me when I was very young. She'd wrap me in her arms and say, "You are my little treasure, Cleo. You're worth more than gold or diamonds or pearls. I will guard you with my life."

"Am I still your treasure?" I ask quietly, afraid to speak, not wanting her to go away. And the sense I get is that she is affirming this. I am *still* her treasure. I will *always* be her treasure.

"I'm so sorry," I tell her through a new set of tears. And this is not the first time I've said this to her, although this is the first time it has seemed that she could hear me. "I'm so very, very sorry for that awful night, Mom. I would give anything to take it back. I would rather have lost my life than to have lost you. I love you, Mom. I will always love you."

And then I get the sense that she's saying the same thing to me—that she loves me still and always will . . . that I will always be her treasure. I have no doubt that my mother has forgiven me . . . that she is safe . . . and happy.

Wrapped up in the warmth of that sweet comfort, I fall asleep on the pink velvet couch, sleeping more soundly and peacefully than I've slept since her death.

···[CHAPTER 21]·················

**D**aniel goes with me to the dress rehearsal on Friday night. I try to talk him out of it, saying he should wait until tomorrow, but he insists that he wants to watch me dance both tonight and tomorrow, and so I give in.

"You were wonderful," he tells me afterward. "Beautiful."

"Thanks." I don't bother to tell him the places where I messed up or that I hope to do better tomorrow. Instead I just bask in his praise.

"You could probably dance professionally."

I laugh. "Oh, I doubt that."

"Wouldn't you want to?"

"I'm not sure. It takes a lot of work and devotion."

"Will you continue dancing in college?"

"I'll keep taking dance, just to stay in shape. And who knows, I might even major in it. But not to dance professionally. Although I think it'd be fun to teach dance someday."

"Have you heard from your dad?" He pulls into the parking lot of a new sushi restaurant. Daniel asked me earlier this week to pick out a place I wanted to eat at tonight, because tomorrow night, Aunt Kellie and Uncle Don plan to take me to their favorite steak house to celebrate after the recital.

"I think my dad's still giving me the silent treatment," I admit as we walk up to the restaurant.

Daniel shakes his head. "I just don't get that."

"I hurt him," I confess, "badly."

"Even so."

After we sit down at our table, I change the subject by bringing up graduation. As class president, he has to deliver the final speech. "How's it coming?"

He groans. "I don't know. I'm on about my fiftieth draft."

"Just speak from your heart."

"I want to say something memorable."

So while we eat sushi, I try to help him remember events in high school that seem memorable to me. But the more we talk, the more I realize that memory is subjective. And I'm certain that my most memorable thing during all of my high school years will always be the death of my mother.

· · · · · · · · · ·

Because Madame Reginald wants the dancers there an hour early, I decide to drive my mom's car and meet up with my aunt and uncle later. This car is slowly feeling more and more like my car . . . and yet I can feel my mom's presence in it, too. As I pull out of the driveway, I know I'm about to have another "conversation" with her.

"I so wish you were here with me tonight," I say as I drive toward town. "I would give anything to have you at the recital, Mom. Aunt Kellie keeps telling me that you *will* be there. So I'm going to believe that. I'm going to look out into the audience and believe that you're out there. And just between you and me, Mom, I'll be dancing for you tonight. I hope I make you proud."

It's hard not to bring up the hurt I feel knowing my dad won't be there. But if she really is listening, and I hope she is, I don't want to burden her with this.

"Tonight is for you, Mom. *All for you.*"

And as I dance later, I can feel my mom's presence, not somewhere out in the audience but right there on the stage with me. I feel her warmth, I feel her love, I feel her pride. So much so, that by the time I take my final bow, my eyes are blurred with tears.

And when I see someone coming toward me on the stage, with a huge bouquet of red roses, I think it's Daniel and I can't believe he'd do this. But as the man gets closer, I'm shocked to see that it's my dad.

Like me, his eyes are filled with tears. With the audience still clapping, he hands me the bouquet, then hugs me tightly to him. "I'm so sorry," he says into my ear. "I've been a stubborn fool. Please forgive me."

Before I can respond, he steps back, moving away from me and waving his hand toward me like I'm supposed to be the star. Feeling awkward, I take another bow, and the audience continues to clap. Naturally, they have no idea what's going on up here between my father and me. Their applause is simply to show appreciation for all the dancers, who are coming back out to take their bows.

Finally, the curtain falls, and Madame does her usual speech, praising us for all our hard work this year. Then we present her with our appreciation gift, which is usually picked out by my mother, but this year Faith's mom took care of it.

As soon as I can, I slip away from the stage to seek out my dad. I can't believe he came tonight — or that he brought me roses and actually apologized to me. As soon as I find him, I hug him again.

"I'm the one who's sorry," I say as I lead him to a quiet corner. "Please, please, forgive me."

He nods. "I already have." He retrieves a handkerchief and wipes his eyes. "Your mother paid me a visit the other day."

"*What?*"

He makes a crooked smile. "I woke up from a nap, and it was almost like I could hear her talking to me, telling me to *shape up*. She reminded me how precious you are, *her little treasure*."

"She said *that?*"

He shrugs. "Something like that. Anyway, she got my attention. And I realized, not for the first time, that I am partially to blame for what happened. I was a negligent husband to your mother, Cleo. If I'd been around more, she might not have obsessed so much over you and your safety. And if I'd been more available to you, well, things might've gone differently. You might not have done what you did. Your mother might not have done what she did. I have to take a good portion of the responsibility in all this."

"But you can't blame yourself for other people's choices," I tell him. "That's something I've been learning. We can only control ourselves."

He nods. "That's true."

Then I tell Dad about how I felt that Mom was here tonight, how she was with me on the stage.

"Well, you were always her little treasure, Cleo." He touches my hair. "I suspect your mother is always going to be nearby . . . protecting you."

"Kind of like an angel?"

He smiles. "Maybe so, Cleo. Knowing your mother, she'd be doing everything possible to be near you. I wouldn't be surprised if she made an attempt to talk God into letting her become your own personal angel." He chuckles. "Not that it's possible, but if anyone could pull that off, it would be your mother."

And it could be my imagination, but sometimes it does feel like she's with me. Like when a warmth comes over me for no particular reason, I imagine it's my mother nearby. Aunt Kellie says it's because my mom loved me so much that she planted a bit of herself inside of me. Whatever it is, I appreciate it.

There have been moments, those special times when a girl needs her mother by her side, that I felt Mom right there with me. When I graduated, she was there. When I turned eighteen, she was with me. I felt her looking on as I blew out the candles on the lopsided chocolate cake Aunt Kellie made.

I'll always miss Mom's physical presence, her hugs, her smiles . . . even her hovering. And I'll always regret making a bad choice that day. But my consolation is that someday I will be with her again. Someday she will welcome me into heaven.

Until then, and with God's help, I will try to make her proud.

1. What was your first impression of Cleo? What could you relate to about her? Or if you didn't relate to her, explain why.

2. Lola was a good friend to Cleo. What are the traits you appreciate most in a friend?

3. What was your first impression of Cleo's mother? How does she compare to your own parents or guardians? Describe what you think an ideal parent might be like.

4. Describe how you felt when you read about Cleo's mother's death. How do you think you'd feel if you lost someone close to you? What emotions do you think you might experience? Anger? Guilt? Sadness? Fear? Explain.

5. Were you surprised by Cleo's reaction to her mother's death? Did it seem realistic to you?

6. Cleo started off very resentful of Aunt Kellie, yet it was this same aunt who proved to be Cleo's closest friend during her ordeal. Have you ever had a person like that in your life — someone you disliked initially but grew to love eventually? Describe a situation like that.

7. Were you surprised when Cleo became addicted to illegal prescription drugs? Why or why not?

8. Cleo believed that she could never tell anyone her horrible

secret, yet her secret was slowly killing her. Have there been times in your life when you kept a painful secret? Did you eventually tell someone? If so, did it help you to get things out into the open?

9. Why do you think it took Cleo's dad so long to "come around," as Aunt Kellie liked to say? Describe how you felt when he showed up at her recital.

10. A lot of factors (including God, Aunt Kellie, counseling, journaling, friends, ballet, a grief group) helped Cleo to work through her guilt and grief. List the ones you think were most valuable in order of their importance.

11. If you've ever been in a dark and hopeless place, what sources did you rely on for your strength?

MELODY CARLSON has written more than a hundred books for all age groups, but she particularly enjoys writing for teens. Perhaps this is because her own teen years remain so vivid in her memory. After claiming to be an atheist at the ripe old age of twelve, she later surrendered her heart to Jesus and has been following him ever since. Her hope and prayer for all her readers is that each one would be touched by God in a special way through her stories. For more information, please visit Melody's website at www.melodycarlson.com.

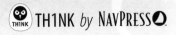

# MY LIFE IS **TOUGHER** THAN MOST **PEOPLE REALIZE.**

I TRY TO
KEEP EVERYTHING
IN BALANCE:
FRIENDS, FAMILY, WORK,
SCHOOL, AND GOD.

IT'S NOT EASY.

I KNOW WHAT MY
PARENTS BELIEVE AND
WHAT MY PASTOR SAYS.

BUT IT'S NOT
ABOUT THEM.
IT'S ABOUT ME...

ISN'T IT TIME I
OWN MY FAITH?

THROUGH THICK AND THIN, KEEP YOUR HEARTS AT ATTENTION, IN
ADORATION BEFORE CHRIST, YOUR MASTER. BE READY TO SPEAK
UP AND TELL ANYONE WHO ASKS WHY YOU'RE LIVING THE WAY
YOU ARE, AND ALWAYS WITH THE UTMOST COURTESY. 1 PETER 3:15 (MSG)

www.navpress.com | 1-800-366-7788   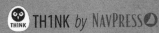 THINK  TH1NK *by* NAVPRESS

# The Message Means Understanding

*Bringing the Bible to all ages*

*T*he *Message* is written in contemporary language that is much like talking with a good friend. When paired with your favorite Bible study, *The Message* will deliver a reading experience that is reliable, energetic, and amazingly fresh.